SKELETONS

Chisto Healy

SLASHIC HORROR
PRESS

Edited by David-Jack Fletcher

Interior design by Cat Voleur

Cover image by Christy Aldridge of Grim Poppy Design

The Survivor first published in *Price Slashers* in 2024 by Slashic Horror Press. Mean to the End as a Means to an End first published in 2024 in *We're Still Here* by Gloom House Publishing. Skeletons first first published in 2024 by Chisto Healy.

Other titles by Chisto Healy

For David-Jack Fletcher for not just supporting my books and my journey but supporting me and being a true friend. Go buy his books.

CONTENTS

THE SURVIVOR

ONE

June 16th, 2023, 2:45 p.m.

PAULIE PAISANO TOOK THE rugelach out of his mouth and put it down on the greasy wax paper sitting on the dashboard of his police car. When he did, flakes of dried glaze fell from his olive-skinned, square chin onto his lap. Beside him, his partner, Sal "Guido" Corelli, looked at him with disgust. "Who the fuck taught you how to eat? Use a fucking napkin for Christ's sake. I think your uniform eats more than you do. *Disgraziato*."

"Shut up. Look," Paul said, pointing forward. "I think that's Melissa Goldstein."

3

Sal looked out the front windshield in an effort to see what his partner was pointing at. "The broad from the deli with the press-on nails and the hoop earrings?"

"No, you schmuck. The one that's been missing."

"Oh shit," Sal said, looking again. Then he saw the woman. "Oh shit. Paulie, she looks fucked up."

Across the parking lot, past the many parked cars and busy speed-walkers, a woman had come out the front door of Price Slashers. She looked like a wild animal—wide brown eyes shining with madness. Her long, sandy-blonde hair was matted with clumps of dried blood and some kind of mud or residue. She was wearing the same red shirt and gray, hooded sweatshirt that she was last seen in the day she disappeared—a week ago—only now the clothes were spattered with blood, just like her screaming face. She was looking around like she didn't know where she was. Just screaming. The other shoppers were looking at her with a mixture of fear and annoyance. She raised bloody hands and started swatting at them.

"This is big," Paulie said, wiping his mouth with the back of his hand. "I think we gotta go get her."

The two officers opened their car doors and got out.

Before they could even close the doors, the wild-looking, blood-soaked woman took off at a sprint with a primal scream that made her sound possessed.

"We got a runner," Sal shouted.

"Guido, chase her. I'm goin' around to cut her off."

"Wait, why?"

"Because I'm faster. Just go."

"We're talkin' about runnin', not cummin', Paulie."

4

"Seriously? You're doing this now? She's getting away."

"You're buying the beer later."

"Suck my dick."

"Beer first."

"For fuck's sake. Fine. I'll chase her. You go around." Paulie took off after the screaming woman. Sal smirked and got back in the car. He started it up and sped off, but left his sirens quiet. This was one time he didn't want backup. Finding the missing woman would be a big deal. It could be just what their careers needed.

"Melissa!" Paulie shouted as he ran. "Stop running! I want to help you." The frantic woman didn't stop though. She might have even picked up speed. Her arms pumped and her legs churned and her mouth let loose wild, furious screams. She seemed more like a movie monster than a missing woman. Paulie couldn't help but wonder what the hell happened to her the week that she was gone. Was that her blood all over her, or someone else's?

He chased her through the streets. She had a good head start, and he was getting winded but he wasn't about to let her go. Then she ran diagonally across the highway as she fled from him. Why the hell was she trying to get away? She was the victim, wasn't she? Why was she afraid of the police? Paulie looked both ways and then ran after her. A squad car came right around the corner and slammed into the sprinting woman. It slammed on the brakes but Melissa was airborne. She hit a telephone pole with a dull thud and collapsed to the street in a broken heap.

"Fuck!" Paulie screamed as he ran to her. The police car stopped right there in the middle of the street and Sal got out.

"Shit. I was trying to cut her off, not kill her."

Paulie shot him an angry glare and shook his head. "I meant to go around on foot, Guido, not in the fucking car."

"I know, but I'm not as fast as you. I thought we established that."

"Fuckin' A, you better hope she's alive. Call a bus."

Paulie approached the broken woman and squatted down before her. The way her legs were bent, she looked more like a dummy than a real person. *This can't be good*, he thought. *We're gonna wind up in a world of shit. Goddamn Guido.*

He leaned closer, grimacing at her broken leg, the jagged, splintered bone tore through the meat of her calf like a bony finger pointing accusations at him. He swallowed the lump that formed in his throat, then he reached for her neck to feel for a pulse. When he leaned in, her mouth opened, her chest bent and she gave a strained, haggard gasp. Paulie jumped backward and fell onto his rump. He could hear Sal laughing behind him.

"Bus is on the way," Sal told him.

Paulie ignored him. "An ambulance is on the way," he said to Melissa. "We're gonna get you help, okay? Just hang tight."

She stared back at him with those wild, crazy eyes, and then reached up. Grabbed his sleeve with her bloody hand. There were some brown stains, days-old blood, some dried but fresher, a maroonish shade, and some glistening bright red, that was brand new and courtesy of the police department. She didn't speak. She just stared at him, stared right into his eyes and something about the woman scared Paulie, scared him *a lot*. Nervous, he patted the hand that gripped him. "Help is on the way," he said.

Even as he said it, he could hear the sirens of the ambulance in the distance. He just hoped she didn't die. Paulie couldn't bring himself to meet her intense gaze. He averted his eyes and sighed. *I gotta call this in. They're gonna want to take that Price Slashers apart. Hell, what if the killer was still in there and got away while we were chasing Melissa? Captain is gonna have our asses nailed to the wall. Fuck.*

"Sorry, Paulie. I fucked up," Sal said from behind him.

"Why couldn't you just do what I said?"

"I don't do what anyone says. If I did, I'd still be married. Here comes the bus."

"Alright. Now call it into home. They're gonna wanna find out why she came running out of Price Slashers. I doubt she was freaked out by how good the sales were."

"That'd make a hell of a commercial."

Paulie sighed again. He looked back at the woman. Her crazed brown eyes had fallen closed, but her hand was still fixed tight to his uniform. "Just call it in," he said, "and hope we don't get fired."

Two

P AULIE SCRATCHED AT HIS face like he used to when there was a beard there. He looked at the man standing before him. Sanchez was a short man, but a big presence, preceded by his reputation. His tanned face was scowling past the steam rising from a cup of coffee. "So you saw her come running out bleeding and you decided to chase her down and hit her with your car. No one bothered to secure the business? Keep everyone here? Not run over the missing woman?"

Paulie frowned and looked away. "She was my first priority. She was screaming like a wild animal and just took off running. If Guido didn't hit her, someone would have."

Sanchez shook his head and then blew at his coffee and took a sip. "Just go on, Paulie. Let the brass sort it."

"But I can help," Paulie said, meeting the man's eyes once more.

"Haven't you helped enough already?"

"I used to be a detective, Rick. Come on."

"You *used to be,* and aren't anymore, for a reason. Look at how much you just fucked up as a beat cop. Get outta here."

"You know what got me demoted wasn't about the job I did, Sanchez. You're a great detective but another pair of eyes wouldn't hurt. Please."

The shorter man chewed on his lip. He sighed, sipped his steaming coffee, cursed and spit it on the concrete at his feet, then wiped his mouth with the back of his hand. "Ten minutes. If I get caught letting you poke around a crime scene, it's my ass. I don't want to be on the beat with you."

"Got it."

Sanchez cursed as he walked away and headed into Price Slashers. Paulie nodded. He took a deep breath and smoothed his uniform as he exhaled it. He wished Guido could be with him. Sure, he fucked up today, but he was a good cop. He was never a detective though, and he'd already gone to face the music with the captain. Paulie knew he shouldn't linger long or Rick Sanchez would rethink his decision. He walked quickly.

When he got inside, it was strange. It certainly didn't look like a crime scene. It looked like every Price Slashers he'd ever been in, minus the customers. The produce was stacked high. The shelves were stocked to the lip so they looked fuller than they were. The tiles were both cracked and glossy. Every third or fourth fluorescent light flickered and fluttered as it neared death. Nothing about any of it said a woman just ran out screaming and covered in blood.

Paulie rubbed at his hairless chin again and then sauntered over to Sanchez. "I'm obviously missing something. What do we got?"

"If only you'd missed the victim with your car."

"Come on, Rick."

"We got nothing, Paulie. We got a damn grocery store. That's it. No one even knows where she came from. Anyone still around for us to talk to said she just came out of nowhere and was wandering around looking spaced out. This is New York. They just took a step further back and kept shopping."

"All... 'I don't want what she's got but what she's got ain't my problem.'"

"Exactly. So where the fuck did she crawl out of? I'm not getting my coffee at that bodega by the train station anymore. Once you get past boiling off your tastebuds, it's like someone scooped out the fucking toilet. Swear that guy waters the shit down instead of making a new pot."

"The Jewish bakery over by Gino's has good coffee."

"And rugelach too. You got some on your face still."

"Fuck." Paulie licked his finger and started trying to clean his face with it as he turned and walked away. He left the front of the store and headed down one of the aisles. His eyes followed the products on the shelves, the ceiling above, and the floor below. He was looking for anything that seemed unnatural. When he came out the back end, there was an employee in a white polo shirt and a blue apron pacing in front of a coffin cooler full of fish and fish-related products. Paulie walked up to him. "You guys have a machine room?"

"Yeah, but it's locked," the young man said. Paulie could see the kid had gauged ears that were empty. They probably said it was against the dress code.

"Still?"

"Yeah, Mike checked. My manager. It's still locked."

Paulie nodded. "Alright, well if you had to guess where that lady came out of, what would you say?"

The kid shook his head. He scratched at the back of his neck. "I don't know man. I just want to go home."

"Just throw out a guess."

"Maybe a cooler?"

Paulie nodded. He glanced at the white, plastic nametag and patted the nervous boy on the back before he turned left to walk the back aisle. "Thanks, Jimmy," he said as he went. *Nothing about Melissa said she'd been frozen for seven days. She wasn't shivering. Her clothes weren't dusted with frost.*

Seeing the double doors to the stockroom, Paulie sped up. He hit the doors and pushed his way through. "Christ, there's a lot of shit back here," he said, rethinking his shopping experience. There were thick, wooden pallets stacked high with boxes and loose products. None of it looked neat or organized. He couldn't imagine they were able to check dates or keep things properly rotated. How much stuff did they throw away each month? He couldn't help but wonder. "Fuckin' people starving on the streets, they're charging us an arm and a fucking leg and they're just letting the shit go bad."

"Who are you talking to?" Sanchez said, walking up behind him.

"Myself, God, I don't fucking know."

"Machine room was locked the whole time. I had them unlock it anyway and it's all standard. Nothing amiss."

"I saw her. I don't think you'll find anything in the coolers either."

"So where?"

Paulie shook his head. "She was gone for a week. Maybe she wasn't here the whole time. Maybe whoever took her dropped her here."

"In broad daylight, with no one noticing? I don't buy it."

Paulie sighed. "Me neither. She looked lost and afraid. If he dropped her, it would have had to have been earlier with her unconscious. Then she would have woken up disoriented and confused but where would he have put her that no one would have noticed her until she woke up? This place stays busy. Hell, there's probably forty employees alone."

"Right. Yeah. So? So she was here. She was fuckin' here somewhere, Paulie."

"What about up there?" Paulie said, pointing. In the back corner of the stockroom, above a bunker was a cage with a door that swung open.

Sanchez ran over there. He climbed on some boxes, slipped, cursed, and regained his footing. In a moment, he was up there, pulling himself inside. Paulie stood below, looking up. "What's that cage even for?"

"Seems like stuff people would steal."

"People steal everything."

"Stuff they would steal first." He sneezed and coughed. "A lot of fucking dust though. I don't think they use it anymore."

"Where's it go?"

"Go? It doesn't go anywhere. Four walls. Another dead end. Wait..."

"What is it?"

"I don't know yet."

Paulie's curiosity got the better of him and he started climbing up. When he was halfway into the open gate he saw what had the detective's attention. Sanchez had found a hole in the wall. Insulation was hanging out with a mess of wires Paulie hoped weren't important. "It was hidden from sight by all the shit around, but she definitely could have climbed out of here."

Paulie pulled himself up. He stood and hit his head on the low ceiling. Cursing, he dusted off his clothes. "She came out of the wall?"

"Maybe. I let you stay to help so I want you to climb in there and tell me what you see but don't go touching shit."

"Why me?"

"Because it's full of insulation, man. That shit is fiberglass. It hurts like hell. Why should I subject myself to that when I have a beat cop available?"

"Wow. You're more of an asshole than I thought."

"Alright. I'll buy you a beer later, okay? Just get in the wall."

Paulie sighed but he nodded. He grabbed the sides of the wall and went in head first. He felt what Sanchez was talking about. Even with gloves on, the fiberglass found his skin. It felt like a thousand tiny needles. He was inside a thin alcove barely big enough for a single person. Holding his breath he stepped forward. With each step, he felt nervous. He knew he had to be walking on the ceiling. In his mind, he saw it giving way and watched himself tumble to the sales floor in a pile of plaster and white dust.

"What do you see? Anything?" Sanchez called from behind.

"Nothing yet," Paulie called back. "Wait. There's a door." He approached the door. It was strange, out of place, and ordinary. He remembered that the store had been much smaller years ago before a big renovation. Maybe this had been an old office or something and they cut corners and just built around it without removing it. *Wouldn't surprise me.*

Paulie looked at the door first before looking past it. He called back, "Door's got blood on it. Fingerprints looks like, some other spatters."

"Don't mess with it. I'll get someone from forensics."

Paulie didn't respond. He took his phone out and took some pictures. Then he shoved it back in his pocket and stepped past the open door into the room beyond. Paulie froze. "You need to get in here," he yelled to the detective. "You need to get *everybody* in here!"

Whatever the room had once been, it was now something else. Something unrecognizable. There was a mattress against the wall before him. It was stained with blood and piss and stunk to high heaven. There was a rat chewing on a severed finger still wearing a decorative ring. In the room's corner, to the right of the mattress, was a steaming fetid pile of feces swarmed with buzzing flies. To the right of the mattress was a table full of tools, hammers, saws, wrenches, pliers, knives, even a blowtorch. All the instruments were crusted with blood and matted with clumps of hair and strips of skin. Paulie was willing to bet it wasn't all Melissa's.

Behind the mattress were a pair of shackles that had been bolted into the wall, but worked loose. He could see the holes in the wall and the white dust on the ends of the screws. Paulie imagined it in his head. He saw Melissa on the mattress, chained to the wall. She struggled and fought, pulling over and over until the chains did come loose. Then she scrambled to the tools and used them to get the shackles off, dropped them by the mattress, and ran.

"Unbelievable." Sanchez entered the room. "We've been finding bodies for months, and he's been keeping these girls in the goddamn grocery store the whole time?"

Paulie turned around to see what the back side of the room contained. In the corner behind him was a white, ten-gallon bucket full of scraps. There were scalps, teeth, fingers, and toes, and god-knew-what-else beneath them. He wasn't about to reach in there and dig through it. He put his fist to his mouth to keep from getting sick. "I think more than prices were being slashed in here, Rick."

"The smell alone is enough to kill you," Sanchez said back.

Paulie turned to face the other man and something squished under his foot. He looked down. Saw it jutting out from the side of his shoe. A human tongue. "Shit."

Sanchez walked over and patted him on the shoulder. "Alright. Look, you did good Paulie, but I need you to go. You were right. I gotta get everybody in here."

"Maybe you can tell the captain I helped you find it, help me get my old job back?"

Sanchez frowned. "I can't, man. If I did that, I'd be telling on myself that I let you look around and play detective. I'd get myself in trouble."

"Word around the lockers is you *enjoy* a good spanking."

"From a stripper, Paulie, not from our captain. Seriously, you gotta go. Take some pictures on your phone if you want. I won't report it, but then you're done and gone."

Paulie nodded his understanding. "You're still buying me that beer," he said, as he started taking pictures of everything in the room.

THREE

P AULIE GOT HOME AND felt exhausted. The day had been a lot. He crossed the foyer, the living room, and went right to the kitchen where he opened the fridge and took out a beer. "How was your day? Fuck anybody?" his wife said with an icy tone. She didn't look up from the sink, scrubbing hard on dishes and slamming them into the rinsing sink.

"Can we please not do this today?" he said as he opened the beer and took a sip. "You can attack me again tomorrow."

"Thanks for the invitation." She slammed the faucet shut, shook the water from her hands, and stormed off. He looked in her direction but didn't follow. Instead, he pulled a chair from the kitchen table and sat down. Paulie took his phone out and started flipping through the pictures from Price Slashers, even though they disgusted him. He was trying to fathom it, to imagine all the women that were killed being hidden in the walls of the store, tortured and bleeding while everyone shopped and went about their day. *If that isn't so damned New York, I don't know what is.*

His wife stomped back into the kitchen. "If you're looking for dinner," she said, "don't. I didn't make you any."

"Okay, Brianna. I couldn't eat it even if you did." He never looked at her. His eyes were on the severed fingers, the bucket of scalps, the blood stains, and tools with hair and flesh on them.

"Fine. I'll bite. What happened?"

Paulie set his phone down, stole his eyes away from the horror and found his wife's gaze. "I found Melissa Goldstein."

Brianna's eyes widened. "The girl that's been missing all week? No shit. Was she alive?"

"Yeah, but hysterical. I helped the detective on the case. We found where the girls were all being kept. There's so much evidence. Maybe they'll finally catch the guy."

Briana pulled out a chair and sat across from him. "Well, this is good, Paulie. You'll make headlines, maybe get your job back. The world will see you as a fucking hero despite what I know about who you really are."

Paulie shook his head. "No. Captain can't know I was there or the detective will get in trouble. I just wanted to help catch this guy. That's all."

"That's all. You didn't want to help your family though, right? So you could have been the detective on that case if you weren't half gay?"

Paulie frowned. "I'm not half gay, Brianna. I'm bisexual."

"Well, I don't remember that from the wedding vows. I remember sickness and in health and death do us part, not while your husband is at work sucking his partner's dick."

Paulie looked away and drank his beer. "I've said I'm sorry a million times. I didn't mean for it to happen. I already lost the job I worked my life to get. What more do you want?"

Brianna stood up and slammed her palms on the table. Paulie grabbed his beer before it fell. It still spilled over the lip onto his hand. He bit his lip to keep from cursing.

"You think that only hurt you? You think your pay cut didn't affect me? You want to know what I want from you? I want you to go stay with Tom O'Connell and remain my husband where I don't have to look at you until I can get my share of your pension. That's what I want."

Paulie finished his beer, stood up, and tossed his empty bottle into the recycle bin. "Tom doesn't want anything to do with me, Brianna. He lost his job too, remember? A lot of the guys at the precinct made fun of us too. It left a bad stain."

"Imagine that. So, all that *fucking your partner while I was home worried* managed to do was hurt everyone. Hmm. Congratulations. Good for you."

"Okay. You win. I suck. Happy?"

"No. The fact that you suck is what made me *unhappy*, you selfish prick." She grabbed a dishrag from the counter and threw it at his face. Then she turned on her heel and stormed off. Paulie just took the dish rag and set it on the table. He sighed and got to his feet.

Paulie walked to the bathroom, locked the door, and turned on the shower. He stripped down and got in but he didn't bother washing. He just sat on the ground and let the water beat on him. It felt like a massage and helped to ease his tension. It was also loud enough to cover the sound of his tears.

He loved Brianna. He really didn't mean for anything to happen between him and Tom. They were in a shootout. It was bad. Both of them could have died. Afterward, they were trembling with adrenaline and facing their own mortality and deep down they must have both wanted it because they seized the moment. After the first time, it became like a drug, a way to erase the tension, to live with the stress of the job. They fed on each other's bodies and found peace in each other's arms.

It wasn't that Paulie was a gay man in the closet. Brianna wasn't a front. He was very much attracted to her. She was sexy as hell and he still enjoyed rolling in the sheets with her, just as much as he did Tom. Tom was the first man he had been with since he and Brianna got engaged, twelve years earlier. He didn't realize the hole it left in him to go without a man until he was with one again.

He wanted both, and he knew he hurt her. He hated himself for that part, for wanting to have his cake and eat it too. He didn't make the decision to do what he did or to be who he was. It just happened. The last thing he wanted to do was hurt her, and he couldn't go back in time and change it. He didn't know how to fix it.

Now he'd lost Tom and Brianna and his job.

Some nights he thought about suicide, but he couldn't do it. He couldn't do that to his Ma. She said she didn't care who he put his *cazzo* in, he was still her baby. She was always in his corner, no matter what. Paulie knew he'd be killing her too if he ever did that, and he wasn't okay with that, no matter how he felt about himself. Nothing in the world meant more to an Italian boy than his mom.

When he'd finished crying it out, Paulie toweled off, dressed, and went to the couch where his pillow and blanket were waiting. He lay there for a few minutes, staring at the ceiling and wishing he were somebody else. Then he got fed up and got up. He walked to the bedroom to tell Brianna he was leaving but she was sound asleep, an empty glass beside an empty wine bottle on the nightstand.

He sighed and walked out the front door. Not knowing where else to go, when he reached the car, Paulie decided to swing by the hospital and see how Melissa Goldstein was doing. If that lady died, it would be more than he could handle.

Four

WHEN PAULIE GOT TO the hospital, he found Sal sitting in the waiting room. His head was tipped forward, double chin pressed into his chest, and was snoring like he was in his own bedroom. Paulie knew he'd probably been there all day, and he went to go sit beside him. He gave Sal's shoulder a gentle nudge. "Hey."

Sal's eyes flicked open and he jumped. He looked around for a second, saw Paulie, and settled down. "Hey, partner."

"You good?" Paulie asked him.

"I don't know. I guess so. I mean, they said she's gonna make a full recovery, but she's still in the ICU. I just wanna make sure she's okay, you know? Maria and the girls said it's okay. I just gotta keep in touch with 'em is all."

"That's good. You were snoring like a buzzsaw."

"Shit. Sorry." Sal waved to everyone in the waiting room. "Sorry everybody," he called to them. Then he turned to Paulie and whispered, "What about you? You good?"

"I don't know, man. Sanchez found where she was kept. It's bad in there, Guido, really bad."

"Oh, no shit. But that's good, right? Maybe we can finally catch this fucker. How many girls has it been now? I think Melissa would have been the sixth."

"There was certainly tons of evidence. I think it'll probably haunt my dreams for life."

"I bet. Not sorry I missed it. How about home? You okay?"

Paulie shook his head. "I don't think it'll ever be okay again, pal. Worst part is, I think she would have forgiven me if it had been a woman."

"Yeah, well, she was raised Catholic. You know how it is."

"You kiddin' me? Where do you think I learned I liked boys? Fucking Catholic school."

Sal laughed. "I like them schoolgirl uniforms myself. Maria used to wear one when we met, hot as shit."

"I like those too. I swing both ways remember?" He knew full well Sal remembered.

"Yeah, that's right. I kinda wish I did. Women can be a lot, even though I love 'em. If I could go hang with one of the guys and still get laid, I think it'd be cool."

Paulie laughed and squeezed his partner's shoulder. "This is why I love you, Guido. I'm gonna check and see if there are any updates." Paulie stood and went to the counter. He flashed his badge and asked the receptionist about Melissa.

"I haven't heard anything in a while," she said. "You can check with the doctor. I'll buzz you through."

"Thanks," Paulie said, flashing a smile. When the doors came ever-so-slowly open, he walked through. He ambled down the hall, kicking himself for not asking what room she was in, peering into each room as he went by. When he got to the end of the hall, he didn't need to ask anyone. His breath caught in his chest. Tom O'Connell was standing outside a door Paulie knew had to be Melissa's. "How's it going?" He was shy as he approached.

"Well, instead of solving this case, I'm on guard duty at the hospital, so that's how it's going."

"Well, how's that going? See anyone suspicious?" Paulie asked.

"Just you."

"That's not really fair."

"It's not? I lost everything because of you."

Paulie nodded and worked to contain his temper. "You know, I get it when Brianna blames me. It makes sense. But it doesn't make sense for you to blame me when you played just as big of a part in what happened between us as I did."

"Yeah, but you've done it before. I've never done anything gay like that. I think you must have gotten into my head or something."

"Tell yourself whatever you think will make you feel better," Paulie said, his words sharp as talons. "I'm here to check on Melissa. Any word?"

"Oh yeah, right. I forgot it was you. Just another person you hurt. They're actually getting ready to move her out of the ICU to a regular room so I guess she's doing alright, some broken bones for sure."

"Has she talked at all about what happened to her at Price Slashers?"

"Yeah sure. We had a candlelight dinner at Vincienzo's and talked about it in detail. How the hell should I know, Paulie? I'm not a detective anymore, and neither are you."

Paulie tried to ignore the jibe. "Where's Sanchez?"

"Out there in the world doing detective stuff, unlike us, but he don't want you to find him."

"What do you mean? Why?"

"Isn't it obvious, Paulie? He don't want the guys thinking you're *shnooking* him."

"Oh for Christ's sake. You gotta be kidding me. Because I'm bisexual, now I'm trying to bang the whole police force?"

"I don't know. *Are* you?"

"You know what? Fuck you, Tom." Paulie threw a middle finger up in Tom's face and turned around to march back out the way he came.

When he got back to the waiting room, Sal was once again impersonating a chainsaw. Paulie just shook his head. He stopped at the desk again and asked the woman working there, "Hey, they told me Melissa is moving to a regular room soon. Any way you can check the computer and look up which one?"

"Sure, let me see." Paulie waited, drumming his fingers on the counter as she tapped away at the keyboard, his cheeks still burning from the recent run-in with Tom O'Connell. "Here we go," she said at last. "Looks like they're putting her in room 17."

"Fantastic. Thanks a million."

"You bet."

As Paulie crossed the room, he considered waking Sal again but then thought better of it. He just left and hurried to the car. When he got there, the last thing he wanted to do was go home, so he decided he'd take a ride over to Price Slashers. Maybe there was something he missed or some way he could help still. It was better than lying on the couch, hating himself. "Fuck 'em," he said as he started the car. "Fuck 'em all."

FIVE

WHEN PAULIE GOT BACK to Price Slashers he was surprised to find it open for business and not really any slower than usual. "You gotta be kidding me," he said as he parked the car. "Unbe-fuckin-lievable."

He got out of the car and walked into the store. When he got inside, amid the bustle of shoppers pushing carts and carrying baskets, Paulie spotted a woman in a shirt and tie. He walked to her and flashed his badge. "Surprised to see you open so soon."

The woman whose fancy gold nametag said, Diane Richmond – Customer Service Manager, scoffed at him. "They just closed off the section of the back room where the murders happened. You think we can just close down forever? Do people in New York ever not need to work? Not need to eat? Come on. Get the hell out of here before folks think something is happening again."

"Clearly you have a good healthy respect for authority," Paulie said, before walking past her further into the store. He marched his way right to the stockroom in the back. Another employee in the Price Slashers white shirt and blue apron attire stopped him at the doors.

"Sorry, no one's allowed back there," the tall, scrawny youth adorning a band aid to cover his eyebrow piercing said.

Paulie looked at his plastic nametag. "Listen, Christopher, I'm a cop. My name is..."

"I know who you are," the boy said. "Detective said nobody goes in if he ain't with them."

"I don't think he meant me. I'm the one that found the place."

"I was here, bro. Take it up with him."

"Step aside."

The boy stood in front of the door, all hundred-and-ten pounds of him blocking Paulie's path. "I can't let you in. I'm sorry."

For a moment, Paulie considered grabbing the kid and physically moving him aside, but thought better of it. His lip twitched. He nodded and then walked off. Paulie made his way to the bathroom. He opened the door and held it. Then he waited. He saw Christopher come out of the backroom with a U-boat cart full of boxes and drag it to one of the aisles. The moment he did, Paulie left the bathroom, hurried to the stockroom, and pushed his way in. He didn't hesitate. He climbed up and past the caution tape into the cage, through the hole in the wall, down the hall, and into the murder room. It had also been taped up, but Paulie forced his way in. When he did, he was in awe.

Paulie had the pictures on his phone to prove what the room had been, but now that everything had been bagged-and-tagged and cataloged as evidence, it was just a filthy, empty room. They had even taken the pile of shit in the corner, probably to check for DNA. The tools were gone. The shackles were gone. The bucket of parts was gone. The finger was gone, but Paulie couldn't help but wonder if the police had taken it, or the rat. Only the mattress remained, though he was sure it had been gone-over for samples and prints. Paulie walked over and sat on it. *I don't even know what the fuck I'm doing here. If there was anything to find, Sanchez would have found it. His case closure is almost one hundred percent.*

Paulie reminded himself that Melissa would have been the sixth victim of this killer and they hadn't been caught yet. It was worth a look. He was damn good at what he did, and even the captain knew it. It just didn't matter in the end.

Paulie stood and lifted the mattress. He was sure it had already been done but he wanted to be thorough. He looked at the floor first and then the mattress itself. Aside from the stains that he didn't want to think about, there was nothing to find. He chewed on his fingernail. *Come on. Come on.*

Paulie reached into his pocket and took out his gloves. He shrugged them on and then went about feeling all the walls. He walked the whole room. The walls were solid, with a few cracks and spots of chipped paint but nothing spectacular. He saw something above the door that caught his eye. Paulie shut the door and went and grabbed the mattress. He dragged it over but he still wasn't tall enough. *Damn it!*

Paulie reopened the door, hurried back to the entrance to the gate, and waited, listening to someone in the stock room loading boxes. When he heard the door swing, only then did he climb out. He felt the boxes to find one firm enough to hold his weight and then he tossed it up into the cage. With a glance over his shoulder to make sure he hadn't been seen, Paulie climbed back up and took the box with him. He went back to the room, set the box on the mattress, and stood on it. There was a line. He felt it with his finger. He couldn't see it but he could feel it. It was a full rectangle.

Paulie dug a knife from his pocket and tried to scratch over the line. Sure enough, when the paint came away there was a crack. There was a tiny hole in the center, he realized. He shook his head and dug his knife in further, trying to cut the entire rectangle from the wall. Flakes of paint and plaster fell away. He scraped hard until he could get his fingers in there. He tried to pull out the piece of wall but it wouldn't budge so he dug at it more, cursing as he worked. *Come free. I need this damn it. Come on.*

Paulie dug his fingers in again and tugged. Finally, the rectangle-of-wall came free in his hands and he went tumbling backward with it. He hit the ground and smacked himself in the face with the brick. He felt the cartilage of his nose break like he'd been punched by a heavyweight. The blood poured onto the already-stained floor, and Paulie groaned. Through tear-filled swelling eyes, he looked up at where the brick had come from and found himself looking at a camera. "Holy shit," he said, digging his phone from his pocket.

Six

P AULIE STOOD IN THE stockroom next to Sanchez as other officers worked to get the camera down and check the walls for wiring and any other secrets. The stockboy, Christopher was staring daggers at Paulie as he held a paper towel over his broken nose.

"Fuck were you thinking?" Sanchez asked.

"How about *you're welcome* instead," Paulie said, though his words were muffled by his injured nose. "That camera could be actual proof of what happened in that room. It could show us the killer, give us a photo."

"That camera could be from when that was the old manager's office before the remodel. The hole in the brick was tiny and may not have been enough for it to view through. It might be old tech that was sealed up instead of removed by the corner-cutting construction crew that built onto this place. We won't know until we can see what's on it."

"Then how about you do that, then figure out if you should say 'thank you' or 'fuck you' before picking one?"

Sanchez shook his head. "Jesus, you sound terrible. Move that towel and look at me." Paulie was unsure, but he did as the man instructed. Sanchez grabbed the sides of his nose and shifted the cartilage back into place with one swift movement. He turned towards Christopher and said, "Kid, you got oaktag in here somewhere?"

"What's that?"

"What's that? Didn't you go to fucking school? For Christ's sake, these kids these days. The stuff you used to glue your presentations on and shit, kid, like a roll of poster board."

"Maybe."

"Find me some, and get some medical tape from the HBA section." When Christopher stood looking at him, Sanchez threw his hands up. "I mean now."

The boy huffed, but he hurried off. Sanchez shook his head again and looked at Paulie. "You don't gotta be much of a detective to know that kid ain't the sharpest tool in the shed, you know?"

Paulie didn't think he was supposed to answer, so he didn't. "We're close now," Sanchez told him. "We're gonna get this guy, Paisano, with or without you playing detective. I know you're sad that you lost your position, but whose fault was it really? Huh?"

"I just want to help," Paulie said. "That's all."

"Yeah. How noble, *Sir Knight*."

Christopher returned with the requested items. "Is this right?"

Sanchez looked it over. "Close enough," he said. He took the posterboard and cut a piece off with a knife from his pocket. Then he ripped some tape off and stuck it to his fingers. He held the cut piece of board over Paulie's nose and then pulled the tape from his fingers and fixed it to Paulie's face as a makeshift splint. "You'll be good as new aside from the two black eyes. My dad used to do this for me all the time when I was a kid. At home health care you know? We didn't have insurance."

"Yeah, thanks," Paulie said. "I saw Tom tonight."

"You were at the hospital too? *Madone.* You really feel like inserting yourself in shit, don't ya?"

"I couldn't sleep and it was my car that injured her. I wanted to see how she was doing. Is that so wrong?"

"How'd that go?"

"Not great. I found out they're moving Melissa to a regular room, so that's good, but Tom says the real reason you don't want me around is 'cause you're afraid of what people will think, though he said it in cruder terms."

"Ah, sonofabitch," Sanchez said. He threw his hands up again, shook his head, and walked in a slow circle. "Bitter asshole wants to bring me into his drama. Listen, Paisano, that ain't got nothing to do with me. I don't give two shits about who you're diddling, alright. I care about the job and the rules of the job and not losing mine. *Capeesh*?"

"Yeah, alright," Paulie mumbled. "So, any of the labs come back yet?"

Sanchez stared at him for a second. Paulie could hear the man calling him unbelievable in his mind. "No, not yet," he said at last. "We put a rush on it, but it could take days. Unfortunately, that's just how this shit goes."

"Will you let me know if you find anything on the camera? Please."

Sanchez took a deep breath and let it out very slowly. "I've broken so many rules for you already. I'll call you. No texts, nothing in writing. I want plausible deniability if the captain blows his top."

"I'll take that."

"It's all there is to take."

"Fair enough. It's technically after hours, so once this is done, you're off duty, right?"

"I'm not gonna *shtup* you, Paisano."

"No, but you owe me a beer, and if you really don't care what people think, you'll make good on that."

Sanchez sighed. "Yeah, alright. It'll be a little bit."

"I got time," Paulie said, picturing Brianna's relentless anger in his mind. "Home isn't really home since shit hit the fan. It's a hard place to be."

"Yeah, I bet."

Sanchez's phone went off.

He answered it. "Yeah." Then he listened. Paulie watched him, trying to figure out what it could be at this time of night. "You're shittin' me. Alright. Where? I'll get there." The detective hung up his phone and said, "That beer's gonna have to wait, Paisano. They found another body."

Paulie's eyes widened. "I'm coming."

"There's enough rumors about you. That's a weird thing to get aroused by."

"I mean I'm coming with you."

"I knew you would. Drive your own car, just follow behind me. Plausible deniability, Paisano."

"Right."

36

SEVEN

P AULIE FOLLOWED SANCHEZ TO the Atlantic Ave. bridge. Underneath was a common spot for homeless and hooligans alike. It made sense for a body to be found there.

It made sense for the people who found it not to call it in as well. It had Paulie wondering how long it had been there. When he parked and got out, he slapped himself in the face, realizing how bad he needed coffee. He had a feeling though, that whatever he was about to see would wake him right up.

Sanchez got out of his own car and handed Paulie a cup of coffee. "I keep disposables and a thermos for times like this. It's stout though, be warned."

"Appreciate it," Paulie said. "We know he didn't go back to his room in the grocery store, so he must have found somewhere else to work."

"And we know Melissa was meant to be number six and she got away, so maybe he was in a rush to find someone else," Sanchez said

37

back. "That means we have him on his toes. He's getting sloppy. Soon enough we'll have him in a cell."

Paulie nodded to him and looked down the hill at all the boys in blue, photographers and CSI hard at work. "Shall we?" he said, gesturing.

"Let me go first," Sanchez said. He walked past Paulie and carefully worked his way down the grassy hill that led under the bridge. Paulie watched and blew on his steaming coffee. He took a sip, grimaced, and then followed behind.

When he reached the bottom, Sanchez was already with the others, cursing. There were a few words that Paulie hadn't even heard and he was a full-blooded Italian, his grandmother from Naples and his grandfather from Sicily. Sanchez's mother was Italian but, it seemed, cursed a lot more than Paulie's parents. He made a mental note to ask the detective at a better time what certain words meant. Right now he was more interested in what made them come out of the man's mouth.

Paulie walked over and stood next to Sanchez. He was about to ask where the body was when he realized it was all over the place. Cubes of flesh and bone were littered all through the grass. There were wet organs leaking fluid that ran down the hill towards the water. Eyeballs sat alone, staring up at them, fingers and toes scattered around. There were teeth everywhere, and at least the bottom half of a jaw bone that Paulie could see. He watched a CSI bag the heart. For a moment he thought he saw it beating. He shook his head and sipped his coffee. *I need more sleep.*

"Looks like he just put her in a damn blender and then dumped it over the bridge," Sanchez said, moving his foot as he stepped on a piece of the victim that squished beneath his sole.

"If only," Hartman said. He was the best forensic analyst on the island and they were lucky to have him. "The poor *schmuck* that found her is over there. You might want to talk to him." He pointed to a scraggy homeless man dressed in at least seven layers with greasy brown hair and a nappy beard. "But I can tell you one thing for sure already. She was down here for a day at least. This isn't a fresh kill."

Sanchez and Paulie looked at each other but neither voiced their thought. They walked together over to the homeless man. Paulie knew he was a guest here so he stayed quiet and resigned himself to let Sanchez do the talking. He was content just to listen.

"You found the body?" Sanchez asked. The men had wide, frightened eyes. He looked as if he were still seeing it or maybe something else that haunted him. "Please tell me about it. Tell me what happened."

Paulie watched as the homeless man worked to collect his thoughts to bring himself back to reality. He pulled a glass bottle out of his coat pocket and took a big swig of whatever brown liquor it contained. He licked his lips while both men waited for him to speak. "Thought she was new," he said. Tears started running down his filthy cheeks. Paulie moved to squeeze his shoulder but looked at the coat and thought better of it. There was some kind of little mites crawling around the fabric like living dandruff.

"You're safe," he said instead. "Just try your best to tell us what happened."

The homeless man looked at Sanchez and cried. A stream of snot hung from his nose, swinging like a pendulum until it glued itself to his beard, an elastic rope for the mites to traverse his face. He must have felt it because he wiped it with his hand. Then he began pacing and ran his hand through his hair. *That explains the grease*, Paulie thought.

When the man spoke again, he said, "She'd just been sitting there, wrapped in a blanket. Didn't talk to anyone. Didn't try to eat. Hell, she didn't even do drugs. She'd been there all day. I thought maybe something was wrong, maybe she'd OD'd. It happens a lot down here. I went over to try to help her, but when I tried to pick her up... God help me, she just came apart. It was like she was made of fucking *LEGOs* man. One minute, she was a girl sitting under a bridge, the next minute, I was holding an empty blanket while pieces of her rained down everywhere. I've seen a lot of shit, sir, and this was the worst damn thing I've ever seen in my life."

"You did good," Sanchez told him. "I'm sorry you went through that, but you did good. I'm glad you found a way to call it in and get help."

They left the man there and walked back to the body, or what was left of it. "So she was together," Paulie said. "No way he had time to stack it all and wrap it in a blanket without someone seeing and thinking it was suspicious."

"No, somehow he brought her here rigged to blow."

"Well, I can tell you that she's all here," Hartman told them. "We've put it all together digitally and the only thing missing is a single ring finger."

Paulie tapped Sanchez on the arm. When the detective looked at him, he uttered, "There was a rat in the room chewing on a ring finger."

Sanchez looked thoughtful. "You sure it's not here somewhere?"

"Of course not. It could have rolled into the water. Hell, another homeless person could have run off with it for god-knows-whatever reason. But all the other pieces are right here, so it's a bit strange. See, we put a marker by each piece and then logged it into the tablet. Then we made a digital picture of all the parts we found put together and this is what came out. He showed them the tablet. Sure enough, there was a diagram of a human female minus a single finger.

"And you're sure these pieces are all from the same person?" Sanchez asked.

Paulie couldn't believe it, but Hartman actually smiled. It took a strange type to do what they did, he supposed, but even still, Paulie couldn't see smiling. Hartman said, "That remains to be seen. We'll have to test them. It would definitely be interesting if he put enough pieces of different people together to perfectly recreate a human being. My problem with that is, if he was going to do something that intricate, and be that thorough, why would he forget a finger or lose it? It just doesn't feel right to me."

Paulie nodded. Sanchez did the same. "You find anything else?" he asked. "Any blood splatter? Any weapons?"

"No weapons," Hartman told them. "The fluid is consistent with old Wino Bob's story. It seems like when he pulled her to her feet everything gushed straight out below, kind of similar to a pregnant woman's water breaking. Then the outside fell apart. When Bob dropped the head, it came apart too and the teeth fell everywhere."

"Fucking brutal," Sanchez said. "It doesn't fit the MO at all. Maybe this is something else entirely. It doesn't seem like our guy."

"Here's the interesting thing," Hartman said, flashing his creepy, awkward smile again. "We found string."

"String?" Paulie asked.

"String. It was something thin, dental floss maybe. A lot of it dissolved before we got here, but it was enough for him to both keep the pieces in their appropriate places and to take them apart when she was hoisted up by Bob."

"He essentially turned her into a fucking meat puppet," Sanchez said. "What the fuck is wrong with people? How do they even think of this shit? Fuck."

Paulie spoke up. "Were there any clothes or a wallet or anything that would help identify her before the dental records come through?"

"Nope. Only thing we found, also consistent with Bob's story, was a blanket, now covered in all manner of meat and goo. If I gave my best guess, I'd say it was already down here and the killer swiped it from one of the resident's tents. I don't see him being dumb enough to bring one from home."

Sanchez frowned. "Nothing else? Nothing on the ground? A key, a charm, a watch, a ring, anything?"

"There was lots of stuff on the ground. We have no way to know if any of it belonged to her. This is a homeless camp, Rick. There's always tons of shit all over the ground."

"Take it all. I want every bit checked, even the damn cigarette butts and bottle caps, all of it." Sanchez commanded.

"You got it. We're gonna be here a while anyway," he said. He knelt down and used a yellow plastic tweezer to pick a tooth out of the grass. Then he held it out before them.

Sanchez took a deep breath. He looked at Paulie. "Alright. I'm ready for that beer now."

As they walked away, they stopped by one of the other police officers. "Anyone see anything? You talk to all the people that live down here?"

"Every last one. No one saw anything, at least that they can remember. Just about all of them are drunk or hopped-up on something. But as far as they can remember, none of them can recall seeing anyone bring the girl down here. Whoever this guy is, he's careful. He must have watched, canvased, timed it perfectly. They have free breakfasts over in the churchyard every week. Last one was this morning. It's possible this place cleared out for an hour."

"Look into that. Find out, and let me know," Sanchez said.

EIGHT

P AULIE FOLLOWED SANCHEZ AS he pushed his way into O'Malley Flannigan's Irish Pub. Ordinarily, Paulie would have pre-
ferred somewhere more Italian. He and Guido would go to Mama
Parelli's and drink and talk. The atmosphere and lighting were nice
and the music was good. It was true Italian: classic, beautiful. Paulie
understood why most of the guys went to O'Malley's though. It
was run by a retired Sargent and was blue-friendly. These days, cops
weren't as respected as they once were—not even close. Parelli's liked
good Italian boys, but, in truth, that was code for mafia. Lucky for
Paulie, most of those guys knew him since he was a child and ignored
what he did for a profession when he ate or drank there. When he was
there, he was just an Italian boy from the block like the rest of them.
He knew it wouldn't be the same for Sanchez and the others. Being
half-Italian actually made it worse for him in places like that.

Sanchez got a booth so Paulie slipped into the other side of it. The
music that was playing was the furthest thing from Irish. The owner

must have decided to cater to the younger crowd for monetary reasons. Pop dance music blared from the speakers. Sanchez laughed at the look on Paulie's face. "There's a jukebox. What we hear is whatever people choose. It's a wide range. You want something different, go stick some money in."

"Nah. I'm alright," Paulie said.

A woman with a wave of red hair big enough to protect her in a rainstorm came waltzing over with a pad. "Hey, Ricky. What can I get ya?" she said.

"Whatever is on tap and not comparable to water," he said with a grin, "and whatever he's having."

Paulie smiled at her. "Same."

"Alright," she said, tapping the table a couple of times. Then she headed to the bar. The freckled young man behind the counter was the sergeant's son, Kevin. He filled two glasses for her, and she brought them back to the table. "Holler if you need anything else," she said.

"Thanks, Amanda," Sanchez told her. When she walked away, he sipped his beer which left foam in his mustache. For the first time in days, Paulie was glad to have decided to go clean-shaven. He sipped from his own as Sanchez said, "You know, I'm glad you're such a nosy prick, because I'm sans partner at the moment and I need someone to bounce shit off of and talk to about this."

"Thanks?" Paulie said with an obvious question mark. "I think the girl under the bridge was still our guy, Rick."

"Me too. I just don't like it. I don't like when I get to know one of these pricks, get to know who they're looking for, what they plan to do to them, and how they're going to leave them for us, and they up and fuckin' change it."

"You think it was desperation or to teach us a lesson? Maybe he saw that we found his hangout. The news crews didn't wait five seconds to air it, despite being asked not to, but we knew that would happen because they're vultures. Maybe he was angry, lashing out."

Sanchez sighed. He sipped his beer. "That's the thing, Paisano. I want it to be that. I want it to be something like that that makes sense and adds up, but I don't think it is. I don't think it is."

Paul studied him for a moment, took another few sips of his own drink, and then asked, "So what do you think it is then?"

"Planned. I think it was fucking planned."

Paulie rubbed at his own cheeks and chewed on the idea for a few moments. It was better than thinking of home and life and what he was going to do now that he lost both the people he loved. At least Tom was kind enough to leave. Brianna was dedicated to making his life hell for the next twenty years. He hated to think it, but this killer gave him the break that he needed, the distraction. Soon enough he would have to face the music again and hopefully, it would be far better music than they were playing in here, but Paulie wasn't counting on it.

"Alright," he said. "Say it was the plan all along, to drop the girl in pieces by the bay. Why?"

Sanchez shook his head. "I don't fucking know." He turned up his beer and emptied his glass. Then he raised his arm and snapped his fingers. "Amanda," he called.

"What is it, baby?" she said when she appeared.

"Two more."

"You got it."

Paulie looked at his first beer, which was still half full, but didn't say anything. He just took a good-sized gulp from it. They stayed quiet until the drinks arrived and the server left. "Okay," Paulie said. "So we don't know why. Let's focus on what we do know then. If the girl had been brought there already tied together with dissolvable string, then she was prepared somewhere else, and if she was dropped off before we even found Melissa..."

Sanchez jumped in before he could finish the thought. "And if that finger in the damned store belonged to her, then there's a good possibility that our girl in the river had been in that fucking room, tucked away in the wall of the fucking Price Slashers of all goddamn places, being literally taken apart for days."

Paulie nodded. He looked into his glass, swirled around the contents, then leaned back and emptied it. He grabbed the one next to it and sipped. Then he grabbed a napkin and wiped at his face. "Go ahead, say it," Sanchez said. "Say it so I know I'm not crazy. This is why I brought you here. Say what's in my fucking head, Paulie Paisano."

"If the dead girl was taken apart over time by our guy and it was in the kill room that we found, then either Melissa was in the room with her, watching her get cut to pieces and reassembled..."

"Which would explain why she was so wild and insane when she came running out," Sanchez said.

Paulie nodded and continued. "Or she wasn't in that room and came from somewhere else entirely and we need to go back through that Price Slashers with a fine-tooth comb."

Sanchez nodded. "Yeah. Exactly, so you're thinking what I'm thinking. There's got to be another room just like it hidden somewhere in that building."

"Maybe more than one. You know when I was a kid, I used to work in one of those places and there were homeless that would sneak in and live there for a week or two before anyone even noticed them. It's possible with the one room, that Price Slashers wasn't even aware of what was happening, but if there are more..."

"Then we need to get a hold of the manager of that store, the owner, and everyone else that would have access to the floorplan before the remodel and could devise something this fucking sinister."

"There is another *or*," Paulie said.

Sanchez sipped his beer and waved Paulie on with his hand.

"What if Price Slashers didn't have any idea, there aren't any more rooms, and Melissa was in that one but she wasn't watching? There was no stool, no chair. There was one mattress, one set of shackles. You have to at least consider it, Ricky. What if Melissa was the one cutting that girl up?"

"Put that down, no more beer for you," Sanchez said with a shake of his head. "You've lost it. You think the blonde lady that was reported missing a week ago was hiding in the Price Slashers, cutting up another woman and she's behind, what, six murders now?"

Paulie ignored his request and drank more beer. "Well, you heard Hartman, she was put there before Melissa came running out of the Price Slashers in front of me and Guido. We're there every day, Sanchez. If she was watching, she would know that. You said it all felt planned. How planned?"

Sanchez reached up and fussed the top of his head. "Shit. Shit, shit, shit." He slammed his hand down on the table, then apologized to Amanda who he knew was watching. Looking at Paulie again, he leaned against the booth bench. "No. I don't buy it. I don't like her

49

for this, Paulie. I'm going back to Price Slashers in the morning with a warrant and I'm shutting that damned place down, and scouring every-motherfucking-inch of it until I find every hiding place in there. What if there's more? What if there are other girls trapped in there somewhere just waiting to be displayed for us?"

"What if there's not? What if you already have the person you're looking for because Guido accidentally mowed her down?"

"Then the evidence will show that. The DNA will come back soon and hopefully, we can see something on the camera. We'll know if Melissa is the victim or the killer."

"Unless the camera is from the old Price Slashers and was sealed in the wall and saw nothing, and the DNA in the room all belongs to the victim we found by the bay. We didn't think anything of Melissa. Hell, she needed surgery for her injuries, injuries *we* caused. She's been long since washed of any blood or DNA that was on her person. The killer is smart, careful. I know it sounds insane, but it's a thought I had when we were standing there, stepping in all that poor girl's pieces, and I can't shake it. I think Melissa orchestrated this because she wanted us to know it was her and to know we couldn't pin it on her. She wanted that power over us. She wants us to watch her walk away smiling and knowing damned well that she's guilty."

"You're right. It sounds completely insane. Let's wait and see what tomorrow turns up. Then we'll go from there."

"Tomorrow is technically today at this point."

"Yeah. We should get some shut eye. I'm gonna need a clear head for what's coming next."

"Sounds good," Paulie said, though he knew he wasn't going to get any sleep. He hadn't slept in weeks without the added imagery of the eyeballs staring up at him from the grass under the bridge, a heart being bagged, the chunk of flesh squishing under his shoe, the bucket of scalps, and the rat chewing on a finger. Only a day like this would leave Wino Bob as not the most disgusting thing he witnessed. Even if he tried, Brianna would be sure to make as much noise as possible when she got up. The worst part was, he wasn't angry with her when she did things like that, when she punished him for his adultery. He was angry with himself, and not even for doing what he did. He was mad at himself for not telling her who she married, not explaining to her who he really was, for just waiting until there was no choice. That wasn't fair and Brianna deserved better. He kept his bisexuality a secret because he was afraid it would scare her off, cause her not to accept him, and now that's exactly where it had left them. He made a huge mess out of everything.

Paulie waved at Sanchez as they headed to their own cars a couple of minutes later. "Thanks for the brews," he said.

"I'm still not gonna *shtup* you," Sanchez said back.

Paulie just shook his head and got in the car. As he started the engine to drive home, a thought occurred to him. Tomorrow, while Sanchez was taking apart the Price Slashers, Paulie was going to do a little investigation of his own.

NINE

P AULIE GOT IN HIS squad car and waited for Sal to get in on the other side and sit beside him. "You okay?" Paulie asked his partner.

"I'm 'sleep soundly' okay but not 'cook myself chicken marsala' okay."

"It's a start. You mind if we take a detour from our normal route today? I want to check on something."

"I feel like you're gonna get me in trouble, and I'm actually not upset about it, so maybe I'm not okay." He gave a wry smile.

"So is that a yes?"

"Whatever floats your boat, Paulie."

"Cool. Let's head downstream then."

"Huh?"

"Never mind. How's the family?"

"Certainly not cooking marsala."

"You really want marsala, don't you?"

"Not if I have to fucking cook it. I'm too depressed for that."

"Are you asking me to make you marsala?"

"I'd offer to blow you for it but after what happened with your last partner..."

"You're a dick."

"So is that a no on the marsala."

"Fuckin' A, Guido. Help me solve this fuckin' Price Slashers thing, and I'll make you marsala for life."

"We're not supposed to solve things. That's someone else's job. We're supposed to arrest people and chase down lunatics. Plus, I'd get sick of it. Where we going anyway?"

"Right up here."

Paulie stopped the car and parked by the curb. "This house on the left, it's a two-family. The right side occupant is the fella that called in Melissa's missing person. I just want to talk to him."

"You think he's a suspect or something?"

"No. I think *she* is."

"Well that's just fucked up, Paulie. I ran her over."

"You might have saved lives doing it. Come on."

Paulie got out and waited for Sal to join him. They strolled up the walk and around to the side door. The front door was for the other family. Paulie knocked and waited.

"There a bell?" Sal asked.

"You see a bell?"

"No need to be an asshole."

Paulie knocked again.

A moment later the curtain moved and someone peeked out. Then the curtain fell back into place. *This fucking guy better not try to pretend he isn't home.*

Nothing.

Another knock. "I saw you check the window, Ralph."

The door opened a crack. It was fixed with a chain. Ralph Marino stared out from under it. "What do ya want?"

"You're not in any kind of trouble, Ralph. Relax. I just want to talk to you about something."

"Boys in blue don't come to talk," Ralph said. "Boys in blue come to arrest or search. It's the guys in suits and nice dusters that come to talk."

"Well, I just left my duster at home today. I promise I have no interest in arresting you. Please. I just want to talk."

Sal sniffed the air. "Holy shit. You're kidding me. Is that marsala?"

"Yeah. I'm making a shit ton of it. I cater."

"Oh, *Madonna Mia*," Sal said tossing his arms up.

"What?" Ralph said.

"He's craving marsala, but he's having a tough week. He's too depressed to cook it."

"*Va fan culo*. Hold on." Ralph closed the door. They heard the chain rustle. Then the door opened. "Come in. Sit down. I'll feed you. You're lucky I made so much extra."

"Thank you," Paulie said, taking a seat adjacent to Sal at the dining room table. Ralph walked away and came back only moments later with two steaming plates.

Sal dug right in. Paulie said, "This is very nice of you. I want to talk about Melissa. Why did you report her missing?"

"Well, she was missing, wasn't she?"

Paulie took a bite of food. It was incredible. He made a mental note to come back here if he ever needed a caterer. "Fair enough. I guess I'm just wondering what made you realize that. What made you say, I think something is wrong, and call the police? Had it been a long time? Did she act strange? Did she fail to do something she did every day? What was the sign to you that she had been taken?"

Ralph shrugged. He went back to work in the kitchen. "I called 'coz she told me to."

Paulie put his fork down. "She told you to?" Beside him, Sal was moaning with delight, not giving himself time to breathe. "Hey, *Gavone*...take it easy," Paulie said to him.

"It's true," Ralph said. "Mel told me if she ever didn't show up to call the police right away. She didn't show up, so I called the police right away."

"I see," said Paulie, taking another couple of bites of food. He dabbed his mouth with a napkin. "The food is wonderful. Thank you again. You ever notice anything strange about Mel?"

"Strange how?"

"I don't know. Whatever comes to mind."

Ralph shrugged. "I don't know. Everyone's strange, right? It's New York. This whole fuckin' city is strange. Mel was no different. She was quirky, quiet, lost in thought a lot, probably has ADHD like everyone these days, am I right?"

"Maybe so," Paulie said. "I appreciate you, Ralph. Thanks for your time and this delicious marsala."

"I'd say anytime, but I'd actually prefer it if you didn't come back."

"No. I get that. Don't worry. We won't unless we have to. So have you been to visit her since she's been found?"

"Nah. We're not really close. Like I said, she told me to call, so I called."

"Got it."

"I mean, don't get me wrong. I'm glad she's alright and whatnot."

"Sure. I get it."

Sal belched loud and patted his belly. "Fuckin' fantastic," he said.

Paulie shook his head. "Alright, Guido. Time to go." He looked at Ralph. "Thanks again for everything."

When they got back to the car, Paulie called Rick Sanchez in a hurry. Before he could say anything, Sanchez said, "Damn camera was a dead end. Nothing on it at all. They said it probably hasn't worked since it was originally installed and was always meant to be a dummy camera to deter shoplifting."

"Shit," Paulie said. "Well, listen to this..." He filled Sanchez in on what Ralph had told him, leaving out Guido's obsession with marsala. "Something's not right with her. You mind if I go talk to her at the hospital?"

"No point," Sanchez said. "She's not talking, hasn't said a word since she woke up from surgery. I've tried, doctors and nurses have tried. We even sent the psychologist in. Nothing. Her mouth is clamped shut. Seems willful to me too."

"Maybe it is," Paulie said, wondering. "But I'd still like to try if you're okay with it."

"Be my guest, but wait til after your shift. She ain't going anywhere."

"Anything on the things in the room? Prints or DNA?"

"Yup. Proof that all six goddamn victims were in that room, Paisano. I'm trying forever to catch this sonofabitch and he's been keeping them in the backroom where I grocery shop the whole fucking time. It burns me. I can't stop thinking about it. I don't want to arrest this s-o-b, I want to kill him."

Paulie didn't respond to that remark. Instead, he said, "You said all six. That means you did find proof that Melissa was in that room?"

"Hell yeah. Her hair, blood, skin. It was all there, man, just like the others. That's definitely where she came from before Guido tried to kill her."

"Hey!" Sal said from the passenger seat. Paulie held a hand up to tell him to save it. "Alright," Paulie said. "I'll swing by and talk to her later and let you know how it goes."

"Yeah, alright."

When Paulie hung up, Sal said, "You really think she coulda had something to do with this, Paulie?"

"I really do. I feel it in my bones, bud. I can't let it go."

"That really sucks."

"Yeah," Paulie said with a sigh. "It really does."

"But I heard him say her blood was in the room. I mean hey, I'm no detective, but why would the killer's blood be in the room? Seems like she'd be smarter than that."

"More like smart *enough* for that, Guido. She knew we were coming. She'd watch us daily outside that Price Slashers on our beat. She already planted the last body by the river. She planted evidence to make sure she seemed like a victim as well. We're dealing with a real psychopath here."

"You could still be wrong."

SKELETONS

"I could...but I really don't think I am."

TEN

I T HAD BEEN A long day. They had two robberies, one mugging, an attempted rape, and a teenage kid took shots at them with a nine-millimeter. Paulie was ready for the day to be over so he could get to the hospital and visit with Melissa. *I bet she put the body under the bridge just to help her alibi. She didn't consider that these days we can figure out time of death.*

Paulie walked out of a gas station bathroom and refastened his belt on the way to the counter. The cashier took a coffee from behind the register and put it in front of him. "Thanks, Candace. Things been okay?"

"As okay as they're gonna be, I guess," she said.

He frowned but nodded. Paulie had been a detective too long not to notice the bruises. "Alright. Just be careful," he said as he scooped his coffee up and headed back to the car. When he got there, Sal said, "I don't understand how people can drink coffee at night. If I had any in the afternoon even, I'd be awake all night long."

"I'm not sensitive to it," Paulie said.

Then a call came in. "We got a 10-16 on Milburne. You're closest."

"On it. Number?"

"2473."

"Got it."

Paulie put on the siren and sped to the corner where he did a U-turn with a screech of tires. As he sped down the highway, Sal said, "I hate domestic disputes. I'd rather almost anything. So many of them have to do with kids. I just think of my kids. I don't handle it well."

"Maybe it'll just be a wife who took too much acid or something, Guido. We don't know."

He took a sharp turn with another screech and raced down the road. "I think that's it over there on the left."

They parked and jumped out. A man was yelling inside the house. "We're on the scene," Paulie said into his radio. "At least one male inside the home. Sounds very aggressive."

They walked up and rapped on the door. No one came, but they could hear the man screaming with rage on the other side. "You did this, not me! You did this! I told you not to back-talk me. I told you to pick up your goddamn shoes but you never fucking listen. Now look what you made me do. What do you have to say now?"

Paulie knocked again. "Police! Sir, please open the door," he called. Then there was a knocking from inside. It sounded hard and heavy.

"Probable cause," Sal said, kicking the door. It took three kicks, but it flew inward. "Christ," Paulie said. Beside him, Sal drew his firearm. "Drop it. Now." His voice shaking.

Before them, a man in a wifebeater tank top stood in the living room holding what looked to be a boy somewhere between ten and twelve in his right hand, and he held a hammer in his left. Thick rivulets of crimson ran down the length of the hammer to drip into the puddle already congealing on the oriental rug. The boy had a glazed look in his eyes and his skull was split right between them. There was a hole in the top of his head that was pumping blood like water from a spigot. The kid hung limp, like he was a pillow rather than a person. The man who held him had spattered blood all over his shirt and face. Thick chunks were caught in the bristles of his beard.

"We need a bus right away," Paulie called in. "We have a child down in critical."

"Now!" Sal yelled. "Do not think I won't fucking shoot you. I actually really want to fucking shoot you."

The man turned towards them and started crying. "I didn't want to hurt him but someone had to teach him. You don't understand how he never listens. I tell him every single fucking day to pick his shoes up and every day he leaves them there. He just don't care. Now he'll care."

"Now he might die, you fuck. Drop the goddamn hammer."

"You can't arrest me," he cried. "This is my home. He is my son. I have rights."

Three loud booms in succession sounded as Sal gave up negotiating and gunned the man down in his own living room. Sal might not have been the fastest but he didn't need to be. He was a great shot and the chunks of brain tumbling down the wall proved it. The man was missing his left eye, just a gaping hole where it used to be. He fell to his knees and then collapsed on his side still holding the hammer.

"Fuck, Guido," Paulie cried. "What the fuck did you do?"

Sal was trembling now. He lowered his gun and let it hang at his side. "I told you I don't handle it well when it's with kids man. I think I need to do something else anyway. Look at everything we saw today, everything we did. It was a fucking kid that shot at us earlier. I just can't anymore, Paulie."

"Well, you may be in a world of shit, Guido. You just fucking offed the guy."

Sal shrugged his shoulder and walked to the boy that still hung limp from the dead man's grip. Blood ran in two lines from his cracked skull past his nose on either side, like two streams rushing by a mountain. He tried to speak and that's when they realized the kid's teeth were cracked and shattered too. Sal wiped tears from his eyes with the back of his hand and said, "I'm not fuckin' sorry, Paulie. I'm not."

"Alright," Paulie said. "Just stay with him. Hang on. Don't say anything stupid, okay? He swung that hammer at you...or no...at me, and I didn't have my weapon drawn so you took him down. Okay?" Sal was just staring at the broken child in his arms bleeding onto his uniform. "Okay?!"

"Yeah. Yeah, okay." He was trying to put pressure on the hole in the boy's head. The ambulance sirens rang through the air. Paulie was pacing. He rubbed the stress from his face. This was bad, really bad. With everything going on at home with Brianna, the wrongness of Melissa's case, and now this, he was ready to explode. He was determined to still go see her tonight even if it was three o'clock in the morning, and he knew it might very well be by the time they got through the paperwork that would result from this mess. There was a wet thunk as another chunk of brain fell from the wall to the floor.

Eleven

P AULIE WAS IN A chair in the hallway, sipping a cup of steaming hot black coffee, his eyes red from lack of sleep and too many tears. A door opened across the hall and Sal walked out. "They put me on leave," he said. "It's just as well."

Paulie stood up and hugged him. "They said the boy is gonna live," he said.

"Good, that's good," Sal said breaking the embrace. "I'm gonna go home to my own kids now. Thanks, Paulie. You're a solid guy. I couldn't ask for a better partner."

Paulie sniffled and nodded, wiping his already red eyes. "Yeah, you too, bud. Go be with your family, get your head straight. Call me if you need anything."

"Yeah, I will."

Paulie watched another partner walk away and he plopped back onto the chair. He started to wonder if maybe he needed a career change himself. Maybe he needed to change everything, move to a new town, meet someone new, fall in love again, but be honest this time, try to find a way to be happy, because this wasn't it. He just felt so tired, so emotionally, mentally, physically tired, and it wasn't going to change anytime soon. It wasn't going to change unless he changed it. Sighing, he took out his cell and called Brianna. "It's been a long day," he said to her. "Sal shot somebody who was coming at me with a hammer. We just dealt with the mess. I still have one more thing to do before I head home."

"Is that thing a person?"

"No, Brianna, it's not a person. This is why I called you, to fill you in so you didn't have to think things like that."

"Well, I'm thinking things like that, so go do whatever. I don't give a shit. Don't wake me up when you come in."

"I won't," he said, hanging up. He exhaled and stood with a stretch. Then he headed out to his car. It was time to go by the hospital and see what Melissa had to say. She may not have responded to Sanchez or the others but he planned to take a different approach. He had a feeling she would respond to him because. At the very least, he would learn from what she didn't say, from her body language, her eyes.

Everyone had tells.

TWELVE

P AULIE TOOK A DEEP breath and entered the hospital. He was hoping with everything he had that Tom was not stationed at the door. It wasn't just because of their history. It was because he didn't think Tom would listen. Paulie knew something was up with Melissa and having someone at her door that would ignore him wouldn't help anything.

He walked to the desk and waited for the woman on the other side to get done with a phone call. She sounded stressed, like she was trying to deal with some irate person who wasn't getting what they wanted. *Please don't let that come out at me, not today. It's been a hell of a day already.*

When she hung up, she glared at him like he had been the one on the phone yelling at her. He showed his badge. "I just need to be buzzed back so I can talk to someone. Thank you."

The woman hesitated there for a moment, still glaring. Then she exhaled her tension, nodded, and did as he asked. The doors came open and Paulie tapped the counter, thanked her, and hurried through before she could change her mind. He walked the halls on the other side until he reached the room. He forgot himself for a moment and sighed with relief when he saw it wasn't Tom at the door. Cop there was a young guy, only been with them a year. His name was Roy. Roy Brown. "Hey, Roy," Paulie said. "How's it been?"

"Well, I ain't fucked my partner or anything."

Paulie clamped his mouth shut and shook his head. "Man, the jokes just never stop do they? This one is just gonna keep on being funny forever, I guess."

"Aww, I'm just fucking with you, Paisano. It's in my job description. I saw it in the last email."

"Probably did," Paulie said. "I'm here on permission from Sanchez. I just need to talk to her for a minute and I'll be out of your hair."

"Hey, Paisano... You know I don't care about anything like that, right?"

"Like what?" Paulie sighed his annoyance.

"If you're gay or whatever. I don't care."

"That's special. Thanks. I'm not gay. I'm bi. I'm gonna talk to Melissa now, okay?"

"Oh, yeah, sure. Hey, Paulie, you ever do both a guy and girl, like...at the same time?"

"Why is that everyone's first question? If you're so interested, Roy, you should try it out. You're young. Live a little. I'll be out in a few minutes."

Paulie didn't wait for a response. He opened the door and went into the room. Melissa was sitting up watching TV. Paulie walked over and took a seat in the chair at her bedside. "How's that leg?" he asked.

Melissa just kept her eyes on the TV.

"Yeah, I was told you're not really in the mood for talking, but that's okay, I don't really need you to talk. I'll do all the talking. You just watch..."—Paulie looked up at the TV—"thirty-year-old sitcoms apparently."

Melissa turned her head and met his eyes.

"There you are," he said to her. "Seems to me, you would want the police to know what happened to you inside that room. Wouldn't you want to make sure the killer was caught and couldn't come back for you?"

She started to look at him again but her eyes flicked away like she thought better of it.

"Oh sure, I suppose you're safe with ol' Brown outside the door there, well, that and the fact that you already know there's no killer coming. Am I right?"

Melissa kept her eyes on the TV screen but her fingernails scratched at her opposite arm.

"I thought so," Paulie said. "It had to be difficult to hurt yourself enough to leave that much evidence, huh?" He paused and waited. She kept scratching at her arms but didn't look away from the TV this time. "Christ, It must have taken a lot of work to chop the last girl up like you did. You know forensics proved time of death was before you came running out of that Price Slashers."

Melissa blinked then and coughed into her hand. She hit the button to shut the television off and then rolled onto her side, pulling her blankets up over her.

"That's alright," Paulie said, getting up from his seat. He walked around the bed. "You don't have to talk. See, I know it was you, and before long, I'm going to prove it."

Ever-so-slowly, she craned her head to look at him. Paulie stood at the door and met her gaze. Then she smiled. It wasn't just a smile either. There was something in the way her lips curled, something in the glint in her eye, something purposeful, something wicked.

Paulie shivered. "Your time is running out," he said. He opened the door and exited the room.

"Didn't say much, did she?" Roy asked him. "She hasn't spoken to anybody. I imagine she doesn't trust us much after Guido ran into her with his squad car."

"That's not it," Paulie said.

Roy looked confused. "It's not? You say that like you know something."

"I do. I just have to get the evidence to prove it. Just keep an eye on her Roy, and watch your back."

"Uh, o-okay."

Paulie left. He was dreading facing Brianna after the day he'd had and wished that she would be asleep when he arrived. He hit every red light on the way, which frustrated him. If she was awake, it was only going to make her that much angrier.

When he did finally make it home, it was dark and the night was full of stars. He loved nights like this. When he got out of his car he looked up and tried to remember the constellations. The first guy he had ever been with, a black boy named Carter from a neighboring high school, used to sit on the hood of his Camaro with him. They would sip the beers they got someone to buy for them, look at the stars and discuss all their hopes and dreams. They would hold hands between them and trace the lines between the stars like a giant dot-to-dot puzzle with their free hands. Paulie had thought life would always be happy like that, that love would remain that way. After Carter went off to college, life proved him wrong. Then he met Brianna and found love again and now here he was, alone, looking at the stars.

Paulie sighed and went into the house. He did his best to be quiet. He didn't see Brianna, so he poked his head into the bedroom. She was sound asleep on her belly, sprawled across the entire queen size bed like a corpse in a chalk outline. He sighed, bent down, and placed a light gentle kiss on her forehead. *I really do love you.*

Then he went out to the kitchen, got himself a beer, and went back outside to sit with the stars again. He sat on the hood of his car like he used to and sipped the beer. Tears slipped from the corners of his eyes as he looked at the constellations shining above.

"Shit."

A thought hit him like a slap across the face and he dropped his beer. It hit the driveway, the shattering glass piercing the silence of the night. Paulie looked at the front of the house and grimaced. He was waiting to see if Brianna woke up, if she came bounding out to tell him what a fuck-up he was. After a few moments, he was hopeful that the noise didn't wake her. He took his phone out and dialed Sanchez.

"You know what fucking time it is, Paisano?"

"Sorry, Ricky. It's important and time-sensitive."

"Alright. Give me a second to go outside so I don't wake anybody else."

"Okay."

Paulie went around to his garage and got a broom and a dust-pan. He worked to clean up the broken glass as he waited for Sanchez to come back to the phone. He was dumping the glass into the trash can that was already sitting out by the curb waiting for pickup when Sanchez said, "Alright. What is it? This better be good."

"Does Melissa have some kind of connection to the hospital? An ex that works there? A baby or parent who died there? A doctor or nurse she hates for some reason? Anything?"

"Not off the top of my head, but I can't say for sure. I'd have to check. What are you getting at, Paisano?"

"Her plan. I think it was to get into the hospital. She knew we'd be there. She acted hysterical, in shock, but it was bullshit, Ricky. She knew Guido had gone around to cut her off and she ran right in front of his car."

"You think she planned to get mowed down and almost killed?"

"I don't think she planned to get hit quite that hard, but she did plan to get hit."

"If she came out and sat down in shock we still would have taken her to the hospital."

"But checked her over and released her. She wanted to be there for a while, maybe to find who she was looking for. I thought the girl at the bridge was left there to give her an alibi but I think she was left there to distract us, to give us something to focus on until she could complete what she set out to do."

"Which is what?"

"I don't fucking know but judging by what she's already done, I'd say it's not going to be pretty."

SKELETONS

"All the victims have been women, so if there's someone at the hospital she hates, I'm willing to bet they're female."

"I fucked up again too," Paulie said.

"Christ. How?"

"I told her I knew it was her and her time was running out. If she does plan to do something in that hospital, I think I just forced her to speed up the process."

"Or if she's innocent you just accused her of murder. Either way, we end up drowning in shit's creek, Paisano. Either Melissa does something crazy at the hospital, or she sues the police department and I get fired for letting you in there to talk to her when the truth is you had no business doing so. Fuckin' A."

"I know. I'm sorry. But when I did call her out, Rick... She smiled at me. It was fucking sinister, man. I'm telling you, it's her. I know it in my bones."

"Fuck. Alright. Where are you now?"

"Home. Outside."

"Okay. Go ahead and head back to the hospital. I'm going to look at her file and see what I can find. Just in case you're right, we need to try to keep anyone else from dying tonight. If you're wrong though, Paisano, I might just kill you myself."

"Got it."

"Alright, go. I'll be in touch."

THIRTEEN

PAULIE RACED TOWARDS THE hospital. He was glad he warned Roy to watch his back. He growled as he drove and banged on the steering wheel as his foot slammed the accelerator. *What the fuck are you up to?*

He was driving through the lot looking for parking and cursing under his breath. When he did find a spot, he screeched into it and slammed the brakes, throwing the car into park. When he jumped out his phone rang and he was so focused on the moment that he jumped out of his skin. He tried to answer it and almost dropped it. After fumbling it, he answered. "Yeah."

"It's Sanchez. You're not gonna fucking believe this, Paulie." Paulie knew it had to be something big because Sanchez never used his first name. "Your domestic dispute that Guido killed was Melissa's ex-boyfriend. Apparently, she called him right before she came bounding out the front doors of that Price Slashers."

"You're shitting me. It was part of the fucking plan? Why would he be so invested in her that he would bash his own son's skull in like that?"

"That's the kicker, Paulie. Kid wasn't his son. He was Melissa's. She dropped him off with that psycho a week prior. Witnesses described her to a tee. He disappeared after school shortly before Melissa was reported missing herself. He didn't live with her. He lived with his dad who was distraught and reported him missing right away."

"And what? That was *coincidence*? No one thought she took her own son? That's the story with the most amber alerts."

"Apparently, she hadn't been in his life, like at all. It wasn't like she had been trying to see him and getting shut down. They hadn't seen or heard from her in years and when they had, she was only interested in the father, Victor. She couldn't care less about the kid, so when they both went missing no one connected the two right away. I mean courts had no problem granting the dad full custody and that never happens. I bet if we looked she even signed away her rights."

"But the boy... Guido said he lived. Jesus, Ricky, he's in that hospital. Do you think she'll finish the job?"

"I honestly don't know, but get in there and make sure she can't."

"Alright." Paulie walked fast from the parking lot towards the entrance doors.

"There's a restraining order and an order of protection in place. She couldn't get near her ex-husband's house. She'd been arrested trying on several occasions years back and then gave up and they hadn't seen her since. He's there though, Paulie. Victor is at that hospital. He's been in a constant vigil at his son's bedside."

"Motherfucker. She didn't mean for the boy to die. She meant for him to live so she and the boy could end up in the hospital at the same time and Victor would have a reason to be there. It was a way to get near him. Holy shit, Ricky. He's the one she plans to kill."

"What about the other girls? Why kill all of them?"

"Because the legend of a fucking serial killer would make it easy to sell herself as a victim. We would take care of her and not question her. We would be busy hunting for someone who didn't exist. It's a long con, a brutally violent fucking long con."

"Holy shit, Paulie. She's fucking mad."

"As a hatter. I'm heading in now."

"Alright. I'm on my way. Be careful. Don't underestimate her. You saw the girl under the bridge. She's incredibly fucking dangerous."

"I know. I just hope I'm not too late."

As Paulie approached the doors they came open, and people came barreling out screaming. "Shit," Paulie said, drawing his gun.

FOURTEEN

P AULIE CURSED. HE WAS trying to get past all the running bodies trying to squeeze their way out the door at once. "What
happened?" he asked as he worked past them. "God damn it. Move."

People were screaming and running all over the place. Judging by
her track record, Melissa had probably done something big to cause
chaos. She was into grand gestures and distractions. She'd proven that
already.

Paulie wasn't even going to attempt the elevator with the mass pan-
ic raging around him. He ran to the stairwell and bounded upwards.
When he got to the appropriate floor, he ran to the desk. No one
was there. Paulie shook his head and reached over to buzz himself in.
Then he ran down the halls to her room. No one was standing guard.
"Fuck."

He opened the door and she wasn't in her bed. Poor Roy Brown
was. He was split down the middle and cracked open like a Thanks-
giving turkey. Even if she had something to cut him with, Melissa had

to be strong to pull his ribs apart like that. Maybe it was adrenaline or whatever hate fueled her. It looked like she had reached inside him and used the contents to paint the room. She made sure to make as much of a mess as possible. There were blood and organs everywhere. Something...a pancreas, he thought, rested in the chair he sat in not that long ago. Wetness ran over the lip of the chair to spill onto the floor, a waterfall of death. "Goddammit, Roy," Paulie said. "I told you to watch your back."

Blood was dripping off the ceiling onto his shoulder. He didn't look up. Instead, he stepped backward and something squished under his foot. Now, he did look down and saw he'd stepped on Roy's heart.

Paulie growled and hurried out of the room. He ran down the hall and saw a trail of blood like a red carpet turning the corner. Gun in hand, he followed it. At the next counter, one of the orderlies—a guy named Sam—who had suffered some kind of terrible head wound which explained the blood, had been dragged to the counter and nailed to it by a pen through the throat. His mouth and eyes were wide, capturing his last moment of terror.

Paulie heard crying and leaned over the counter. One of the nurses was huddled beneath clutching her knees to her chest and shaking like she was naked in a snowstorm. "I know you're scared," Paulie said to her, "but I need your help. The boy. The boy that was brought in after being attacked with a hammer. Where is he? Did he make it out of the ICU?"

The woman looked up over her knees at him.

"Please," he said. "That's where she's going. She's going to hurt a lot more people if I don't stop her."

"He's...in the...coma ward," she stuttered. "They stopped the bleeding and sealed the wounds but he hasn't woken up. He may never wake up."

"How do I get there? Please. I need to hurry. You've seen what she's capable of."

"It's an isolated wing off of the ICU."

Paulie nodded and hurried that way. As he did, people were coming in the opposite direction in a hurry, screaming. He wished he knew what Victor looked like to know if he was among them. He didn't know where the hospital security was, but if they had gone after Melissa, he had a feeling that they didn't fare well. Surely, Sanchez would catch up to him soon and he would have called for backup. This whole situation was a mess.

A woman screamed, the panicked crowd parted. Paulie headed toward the gap for a path through. She had slipped in a pool of blood and went right down into the heart of it. She was trying to get up and kept slipping. She was looking at all the blood on her clothes, screaming. Just a few feet behind her was the source of the blood and the answer to Paulie's previous question. One of the security staff—a woman named Cara who Paulie knew well—had her throat slit wide. Her glassy eyes stared at the ceiling. Paulie looked up. One of the fluorescent lights crackled and flickered.

Paulie knew helping the fallen woman could result in more people ending up like poor Cara, so he apologized and stepped over the mess to hurry back down the hall. Making it to the elevator, he hit the button. He was tapping his gun on his forehead in frustration. They figured it out too late and then he put a rush on her plan. These dead people were his fault as far as he was concerned. His lip twitched and he growled. It was taking too long. A look at the stairwell door showed it wasn't a better option. People were fighting to get in and out of it, screaming and struggling. Paulie wondered how many were going to die from the panic alone.

Then the elevator doors came open and the box emptied out; a stampede of terrified people ran right into him. "Shit," he yelled as he fell.

They trampled over him, stepping on him and kicking him as they went by. Some fell over him and cried out as they hit the floor. Paulie just curled up on himself and guarded his head. His ribs and guts were killing him by the time the flow of people ended. He tried to get up, and panicked people came from the other direction rushing towards the elevator. They plowed into him and knocked him back over, bumped him around, and ran for the open elevator. Paulie got up on a knee, blood running from his nose and one side of his mouth, and he fired his gun at the wall to the outside. He didn't want to hit a person. It did the job and the people screamed and hit the deck, covering their heads. Paulie got to his feet with a groan of pain and pointed his gun toward the elevator. "Everybody out. Now."

Defensive hands shot up, and they did as he said, running out and scurrying in all directions like a pile of roaches when the lights came on. Paulie took their place and hurried into the elevator. He hit the button for the third floor. That critical care unit. That's where the ICU was located and the coma ward as well. That meant it was also where Victor was and where he would find Melissa.

As the elevator moved, Paulie wondered how the woman made it through her own mess. He just about got trampled to death himself. He thought of her running out of Price Slashers, screaming and frantic. He could picture the same thing here. She probably played the part, screamed, and ran, going with the flow. She could have been in the tide of bodies when she slit the security guard's throat. She wouldn't be noticed until it was too late then. She was insane for sure, quite possibly evil, but there was no one that could say Melissa wasn't smart.

When the elevator doors opened, Paulie stepped out, gun raised. Unlike the other floors, things were quiet. There was a bed against the side wall. A nurse was slumped over the patient he'd been pushing in it. A sharpened piece of bedrail that she'd probably worked on the whole time she was here had been driven through the back of his head. It came out the front and went into the screaming mouth of the woman beneath him, tacking them together. Her arm hung limp from the bedside. *Was that the weapon she used the whole time?*

She could have used it to open up Roy, to beat the orderly over the head, to slit the security guard's throat. If that was the case, then it had been abandoned, but he didn't want to assume that she was unarmed. It was just wishful thinking, he supposed.

Paulie moved down the quiet halls past the rooms full of beeping monitors and inflating and deflating pumps, ventilators, and the like. It had a strange sort of rhythm to it. It was nerve-inducing. He followed the signs until he found the coma ward. There were only a couple of nurses on the ward from what he'd been told. If that was the case then they were both here sitting like a child's dolls against the wall, their legs out, and chins to their chests. One had a pen driven far into her eye socket. Her body still spasmed, twitching and jerking like a wounded animal. The other had a faceful of syringes. Needle caps surrounded her like spent shells. It was overkill and Paulie imagined her in a rage fit, screaming and jamming all the syringes she had into the woman's face. He didn't think the injuries would have been enough to kill the nurse. Sure it would hurt like hell, and cause some need for cosmetic surgery, but he didn't think she would die. *Maybe there was something in one of them...or all of them. Jesus.*

Paulie walked past the nurses and looked in the rooms for any sign of the boy and his father. He didn't see them anywhere. Did she take them? No. That wasn't possible. She would have to take the boy in a bed and she couldn't have done that with the mass panic she had caused. She wouldn't have gotten anywhere. They had to be here somewhere.

Then he got to the end of the hall. "Fuck."

They were in the last room. It wasn't good. The boy was in the bed in his comatose state, the monitor beside him showing his heartbeat steady. There was a breathing tube over his mouth and nose. His father was in the seat beside him. His hand was holding his son's but it wasn't attached to his wrist. He was slumped over, his head against the railing of his son's bed. His wrist was bleeding heavily onto the floor. Paulie could smell the gunshot before he even saw the bullet wedged in the bed frame. Melissa must have taken Roy's gun or maybe the security guard's. She blew his wrist clean off.

The question was, where was she now? Had she accomplished what she set out to do and now she was trying to make her way out? No. Everything she'd done had here. She didn't plan to shoot his hand off and leave him there to go on her merry way. This was her hoorah. She would take her time with Victor, take him apart like she did the women she used to build her legendary killer. Then she would kill herself or let someone else do it. In his detective days, Paulie had seen people like her before, people driven by revenge, true psychotics. It almost always went the same. Almost.

The gunshot hit him in the shoulder and spun him around. He crashed into Victor, who fell out of the chair onto the floor. Paulie fell over him and scurried into the corner taking cover between the bed and the table at its side. She was smart in hitting him in his gun arm. He switched the gun to his other hand, but in truth, he didn't have confidence that he could hit the broad side of a barn with that hand. Melissa stepped out from behind the door, gun in hand.

"He's not dead," she said. "He just passed out from blood loss. But he will die if I don't do something to stop it."

"You want him to live?" Paulie tried to raise the gun.

"Of course. I want him. He's mine. He's always been mine. He had no right to leave me like he did. He chose this *shit* child over me." She pointed the gun toward the bed.

"No!" Paulie screamed, but the shot was already fired by the time he got the word out. He was sprayed with the blood. It coated his face and hair.

"It was mercy at this point. Come on. They said he might never wake up. The asshole that was supposed to send him here did a bit more than he was meant to. Just as well..."

Paulie fired

It went wide, the bullet hitting the door.

Melissa cracked up laughing. She took a bed sheet from the dead boy—now with half a head—and tied it tight to Victor's stump like a tourniquet. Paulie didn't want Victor to die, so he waited until she was done. Then he jumped on her back.

Dropping to her knees, Melissa slung him over her head. His back hit the ground hard, a shockwave of pain coursing through his shoulder. The gun fell from his hand to slide across the floor. "How do you plan to get him out of here?" he said with a groan.

Melissa laughed again. She pointed the gun at him as she hoisted Victor up and set him in a wheelchair nearby. "You've seen this place. It's pure hysteria. There's no one on this floor but us. I'll put some nurse's clothes on and walk right on out, dear."

"It's not going to work."

"Shush now. This has been fun but it's over now."

"Your damn straight it is," Sanchez said from behind her. He was pointing his gun and had several officers behind him. "Put it down and put your hands in the air."

"Take one step, I pull the trigger and your buddy here loses his brains. Sure, you'll kill me, but not before I kill him."

Sanchez stayed where he was.

"Do it," Paulie said. "Take her out."

"Guns down and back out of this room. Close the door behind you," Melissa said.

"Even if you get out of the room, you're not going to get out of the building," Sanchez said as he used hand signals to tell the officers behind him to move back out of the room. "The entire place is crawling with cops now."

"Cops busy with crowds of panicked people, trample victims, injured and dead staff. I'll take my chances. Out."

Sanchez backed out of the room and closed the door. Paulie dove up, barreled into her and slammed her into the wall. She moved to shoot him and he grabbed her wrist. He slammed her arm into the wall but she held firm to the weapon. The door flew back open and Sanchez and the others came crashing in. Sanchez slammed his pistol into the side of her head and she still fought. One of the officers wrestled the gun away from her. It took both arms and everything he had. Now she was screaming. It was primal, insane, furious.

It took five of them to pin her down and get her cuffed and still she thrashed. Paulie sat on the ground panting, holding his injured shoulder. Sanchez took one look at the boy in the bed, his skull fragments on the pillow beside him, and he stomped on Melissa's head. Finally, her fight came to a halt.

"I ought to fucking shoot her," Sanchez said, "to do to her what she did to that boy."

"But you're a better cop than that," Paulie said. "Victor's alive, but he needs help fast. He's lost a lot of blood."

Sanchez looked at one of the officers behind him. "You heard him. Find a doctor. Go."

The officer hurried off. Sanchez looked back down at Melissa. "This fucking state banned the death penalty too."

"She'll get life," Paulie said. "She'll rot behind bars."

"After everything she's done, she deserves worse."

"Yeah, maybe," Paulie said, struggling to his feet.

"You look like shit."

"Feel like it."

"I can probably get you your detective status back after this. You saw all of it, had her pegged."

"And missed it from the beginning, helped put her in the hospital where she wanted to be and played into her plan, sped things up with a warning that caused a lot of people to die... No. I don't think so, Ricky.

Thanks, but I think I might leave this whole place, go somewhere else, do something else. I need to start over. Brianna will contest it, but all she wants is my pension. We can work something out."

"Shit, Paisano."

"It's alright. I think Guido had the right idea though. I've seen a lot of darkness, some of it by my own design, and I've had enough."

"You'll be drawn back. Look what you just did after detective was stripped from you. It's who you are."

"Yeah. Maybe I'll be a P.I. somewhere then, work privately, make my own rules. We'll see."

The officer returned with a doctor. He saw the boy and was stunned, held a hand to his mouth to choke back the vomit, and was jostled back into the moment by the officer that brought him. He then ran to Victor and started tending to him. Paulie walked past them and out of the room. On his way out of the building, Tom O'Connell was helping an injured person to their feet.

"Tom." Paulie nodded as he walked by and pushed his way through the doors to the outside. His whole body hurt. His heart hurt too, but change was on the horizon. He walked to his car past the rush of screaming people and emergency personnel and realized Melissa was probably right. In all the commotion, she could have just walked out and gotten away. *But she didn't. At least I did something right.*

Paulie took a deep breath, got in his car, and drove away. He couldn't leave town yet. There would be a world of paperwork to get through on this one, but at least he knew it was coming. When he and Carter used to sit on the Camaro hood together, Carter once said he thought life was like books. Each book was their own story but there was the underlying story that continued throughout, and that was you. Paulie thought about that now and he felt satisfied. He knew this book was over, the cover was about to close, but he was looking forward to starring in the next book and seeing what story life had for him after this. For the first time in a long time, he smiled as he made his way home.

MEAN TO THE END AS A MEANS TO AN END

1

TAYLOR STOPPED OUTSIDE THE house. It looked ordinary—aluminum siding, faded yellow with a green trim and matching shudders. Every time he approached a crime scene, he expected it to look like one, to feel like a place where atrocities were committed. It never did though, not until you got inside. From the outside, it just looked like life.

He sipped his coffee and climbed the steps, patting an officer on the back as he went by. As soon as Taylor stepped inside, the picture changed. The interior of the home held anything but life. Death was everywhere, painted in red and splashed with wild abandon. "Passionate," he said, taking it in.

"Not the word I would use, Conroy," an officer said as he walked over.

Taylor frowned. "What word would you use, Tucci?"

Officer Tucci gave a humorless laugh. "Overkill."

Taylor nodded. "They're the same word in this instance. What do we know?"

"Come on." Tucci led Taylor through the house.

He looked at the splattered walls and ruined paintings but kept looking back at his feet to ensure he didn't step on evidence. When they reached the kitchen, he saw immediately that the window was shattered inward, glass shards making the floor sparkle like it was under a disco light. To the right, a drawer was wide open. Muddy boot prints decorated the off-white tiles, one chipped.

"This is where he came in," Tucci said.

Taylor refrained from telling the man he was pointing out the obvious. "We know what the weapon was? Could the murder weapon have been taken from that drawer?"

"You think he came in unarmed and killed the guy with his own kitchen knife?"

"Could have. Or else, the vic was looking for something to defend himself with."

"Well, if either of them took something from that drawer, it ain't here now. Or at least, uh...we haven't found it yet."

"Alright. Keep looking. Take me to the body."

"Alright, but it's a bad one, Conroy. Jones had to excuse himself while the burritos he had last night excused themselves."

"I'm prepared."

Officer Tucci shrugged. "I don't understand how you stay so calm and stoic. I know you're not like a sociopath or whatever. I've seen you and your uh...guy."

Taylor gave him half a smile. "My husband? Eric? Yeah, I'm not a sociopath. I'm doing a job, Tucci. That job requires a level head."

"And a stomach of stone. In here." The officer gestured towards an open doorway.

Taylor gave another nod. "Thanks."

He left Tucci there and eased his way into the room. "Jesus."

The vic wasn't on the floor or the bed as Taylor expected. That's usually where they were. Not this time. The guy was everywhere. The room had been decorated with him. It was furious, angry, and yet almost purposefully artistic. The smell of blood was in the air. Taylor could taste it on his tongue. Entrails hung from the ceiling fan at the room's center. It was still spinning and flicking drops of gore about the room. Taylor strapped on a glove and reached over to the nearby switch, turning it off. The overhead light went off as well. He frowned and looked at the carpet. It looked like a wet sponge soaked in fruit punch. He feared taking a single step.

Sighing, he backed out of the room. Tucci eyed him curiously. "I gotta bag my shoes," Taylor said.

"I wish I could bag my eyes," Tucci told him.

"Any idea who the vic was?" Taylor asked as he worked to put plastic over his shoes and lower pant legs.

"Well, assuming the vic was the homeowner, he was a guy named Lance Kent, but how are we supposed to know that's him? Sure, they'll do DNA or whatever, but for all we know right now, that mess could be anyone."

"Yeah." Taylor re-entered the room. He looked for anything that could tell him something, a wedding ring, a slice of flesh with a tattoo, a colored eyeball, teeth, anything; but he came up empty. It seemed like the killer took the identifying bits with him. Was that to cover his tracks or as a keepsake because this kill was important to him? There was so much emotion in it.

Taylor continued, going around the room and checking every nook and cranny. He looked under the mattress, under the box spring, under the bed, behind the frames on the nightstand, inside them, in the drawers of the end table and the dresser, under it. He found plenty of the vic but nothing that helped him figure out who killed him. Taylor sighed. He walked over, the rug squishing beneath his steps, and opened the closet.

He flipped through the clothes within. Lance wore mostly T-shirts. They were emblazoned with heavy metal band names and mixed martial arts fight clubs. Taylor figured the guy was just a fan or he wouldn't have been taken so easily and brutally. Unless the vic isn't Lance at all, he thought. Could Lance be the killer?

Taylor continued to pull the shirts from one side of the closet to the other. He stopped at one that had a rabbit on it. It read:

TRICKS AREN'T FOR KIDS. KEEP DRAG QUEENS OUT OF SCHOOLS.

Taylor frowned but pushed the article along with the others. A few hangers later, he found a face. It was loose but cut off intact, facial hair still attached and clamped to either side of the hanger with silver clips. Taylor took a deep breath and let it out slowly. "Found you," he said.

He went back to one of the picture frames standing on the nightstand beside the bed. With a gloved hand, he wiped some of the blood off the picture. His gaze lingered on the face of the man holding a giant fish. He carried the photo back to the closet and compared the faces. Then he put the picture back where he got it and left the room.

Tucci was waiting on him. Taylor said, "It's him. Lance. His...face is hanging in the closet."

"Christ. I've never seen anything like this, Conroy. You don't think it's going to be serial, do you? I would hate to see another one."

"I hope not. It feels too personal to me though. What about neighbors? Anyone see anything?"

"Only one neighbor saw anything, the queer across the street, talks in the girl voice with the hand gestures and all that shit. I can't stand it." Tucci must have just then realized who he was talking to because he cringed. "Sorry."

"Forget it." Taylor took the gross congealed and caked plastic off of his shoes and handed them to Tucci. He walked back through the house and out to the street.

With a sigh, Taylor crossed the street and banged on the door. When it opened, a thin young person stood before him, eyeing him up and down appraisingly. "Well, hello," he said in a sing-song way, "what brings you to my door? Please say you're a stripper."

Taylor smirked. "I'm Detective Conroy. I'm trying to figure out what happened to your neighbor." He flashed his badge.

The homeowner huffed and pouted. "Someone killed him. He was a prick. Who cares?"

Taylor eyed him curiously. "So you didn't get along."

The young man laughed and slapped Taylor in the shoulder. "That's cute. No. He was one of those."

"One of those?"

"Type wears belt buckles big enough to compensate for his lack of balls? Tells his neighbors they go against God, blames the gays for everything wrong in the world. You know the type. Oh my god, he totally beat this kid up last month for 'looking at him gay'. How the hell do you look at someone gay? Am I looking at you gay right now?"

Taylor shook his head. "Do you know who that was? It could be motive for revenge."

"Oh honey, just about anyone would have motive for killing that creep."

"Careful or I might think you did it, yourself."

"I did not kill the homophobe across the street but if you find the guy who did tell him I will suck his dick for doing it."

"Noted."

"My name is Brendan. You want my number? Just in case we need to talk more?"

"I'm married."

"So is my boyfriend." Brendan threw his arms up.

"So I was told you actually saw someone go to Lance's place. Did you?"

"Yup. Didn't get a look at him but he ran by fast all dressed in black like a ninja or some shit." He laughed. "Then there was glass breaking and I remember thinking, 'I hope that ninja kills him.'"

"Well, it seems he did. Which direction did he come from?"

Brendan pointed. "I couldn't see his face but it was definitely a guy unless she was stuffing her pants. I suppose they may not have identified as a guy. That was insensitive of me. I should never assume gender. Fuck. I'm sorry. I'm just horny and not thinking straight."

"It's fine. Killer has a penis. Got it. Anything else I should know?"

"That you are fine but you need to lighten up."

"You're not the first to say that. Did you see the guy leave?"

"Nope, but I mean I wasn't looking for him. I saw him go in and I went back to watching Walking Dead. Oh no wait, I made popcorn first."

Taylor sighed. "Alright. Thanks." He walked back across to the crime scene and met Tucci on his way out the house. "Killer was well endowed, dressed all in black, and ran around the side with speed and purpose. He came here with the intent to kill."

"Prints turned up nothing. Took samples of all the blood we could in case some of it isn't the vic's."

"Neighbor said Lance beat someone up last month, a hate crime. See if you can find out who that was. Maybe it will lead somewhere."

"You got it. Hey, are we good?"

"We're good. I'm gonna get an address and visit Lance's folks. Maybe they know about some enemies. Keep looking for that murder weapon."

11

TAYLOR SAT IN HIS car staring through the driver's side window at a huge white Mediterranean-style house set back on a well-manicured lawn with large decorative hedges and a variety of vehicles in the driveway. Taylor's eyes were on the house but his attention was on the phone in his hand. "It was bad, Eric, worse than I've ever seen."

"Guy's name was Lance Kent. He beat a kid last month for looking at him gay. You hear anything about that?"

"Someone killed Lance Kent? That guy is a menace, Tay. Was. He would go down to the Bird Cage just to heckle people for existing. I can't say I'm sorry to learn he's gone. I think the kid you're talking about was Gary. He's a nice kid, told us to stop hating Lance and kill him with kindness. He just kept looking over. I don't know if he was just curious or if Lance did it for him, but he kept looking and Lance didn't like it apparently. He took his pool cue and beat the boy to nothing. I think he's still in the hospital if you want to visit him."

"Jesus, Eric. Why the hell wasn't Lance behind bars? He might still be alive if he was."

"That seems more like a question I should ask you than the other way around. Honey, you should let this one go. Let one of the MAGA hat boys handle it. There's plenty in the department. You shouldn't be on this one."

Taylor frowned. "I *am* on it, and being a prick doesn't mean he deserved what he got. He wasn't killed, Eric. He was destroyed." When there was silence on the other end, Taylor sighed. "Were you there that night? With Gary?"

"What, am I a suspect now?"

"Of course not. I just thought if you saw him hurting one of our own, beating him like that, it would explain the venom. It's not like you."

"Yeah. I was there. Worked ended early. Samara and I went for a drink. You were in New Jersey visiting your brother. When you got home I wasn't in a rush to fill you in on the bad stuff. I was happy to see you. We went to that falafel place."

Taylor nodded. "I remember. You did seem off, emotional, but I thought it was because you missed me."

"It was... Partly. Tay, the cops came and said that Lance had too much to drink. They drove him home. He put Gary in the hospital. His face... It haunts me. Gary was pretty. Not anymore, probably never again. People told his parents to sue the department but they said this was his fault for going against God and running with those terrible people. They're blaming their own son for getting the shit beaten out of him."

"I guess I can cross them off the suspect list. I'm sorry I wasn't there for you that night, honey. It sounds really traumatic."

"It was."

"I'm also sorry that I have to go now but I promise to rub your back when I get home. I'll bring takeout, whatever you want."

"You're really gonna keep working this case?"

"It's my job, Eric."

"Well, it could have been literally anyone. Why not go to the Bird Cage? Ask all our friends. I'm sure they'll love that."

Taylor sighed quietly. "I'll see you when I get home, love."

Eric huffed. "Fine. I want Indian." He hung up.

Taylor frowned and stuffed the phone in his pocket. It was time to see what Lance's parents had to say and he was dreading it. Kids aren't born full of hate, they inherit it. He got out of the car and made his way past half a dozen cars worth twice as much as his on his way up the driveway. Lance came from money, that was for sure. It made the politics make more sense too. The wealthy tended to be conservative in his experience.

When Taylor made it to the door, he knocked hard. The house was huge and he wanted to make sure someone heard him if they were on the other end. Time passed and he was almost about to turn and head back to the car when the door finally opened.

"What the hell do you want? Banging like you're the damned police," a woman said as she ripped the door open.

"I am." Taylor showed his badge and identification. "May I come in?"

"What's this about?"

"It's about your son, Lance, ma'am. May I please come in?"

The woman shook her head defiantly. "That boy went wrong. He ain't welcome here and I told him that to his face. Whatever the son of a bitch did, it has nothing to do with me. His father tried to set him straight, but it did no good. Listening to the two of them fight all the time is how I started drinking. Now, if you don't mind, I have to tell the cook what want her to make for our company tonight."

Taylor raised his eyebrows, taken aback by her aggression. "Mrs. Kent, Lance is dead."

She looked like she'd been slapped. He could tell she was trying not to show her true emotions. She dabbed at the corner of her eye with a handkerchief. "Well, that's where the Devil's path leads, isn't it?" she said quietly. "I really must be going. Is there something else you need?"

Taylor bit back his retort. "I need to know who might have killed him, ma'am. Did your son have enemies?"

"Clearly, I wouldn't know. I told you he wasn't welcome here."

"Is your husband home? Maybe I can speak with him while you take care of your event coordinating."

"You think I didn't catch your sass there? I'm allowed to react however I want to my own boy's passing. He was my flesh and blood, not yours, and yes, his father is home, but no, he will not be talking to you about that sinful son of his. Bad enough I have to tell him, Lance is gone and there's no chance of him being saved anymore. He's the Lord's problem now."

Taylor put a hand to his mouth. He took slow deep breaths. "I see. Can you tell me what it was that caused the falling out between you and Lance?"

"No, I cannot. That's family business."

"Where were you and your husband last night?"

"Are you interrogating me? How dare you? You have some god-damned nerve. Get away from my house. Get a warrant if you want more. Jesus. Horrible."

Taylor was still standing on the steps when she slammed the door in his face. He felt like he might have been in more shock than he was when he saw the crime scene. This whole case was built on anger. It was coming from every direction. It was a lot to handle. He was beginning to wonder if he should excuse himself from this case after all. Taylor turned and headed back towards the car. He froze when he heard gunshots.

Taylor turned and sprinted back up the steps. When he reached the door, he didn't bother with knocking and he just pushed it open. As he did he heard a scream tear down the hall like a perp trying to escape. Taylor ran after it. He took his gun out as he ran. The boom of gunfire continued.

He felt like he was running through a neighborhood rather than a house. Taylor didn't understand how people could live this way. Everything was so far from everything else, including the people. It had to create distance.

He burst through into a den of sorts with a puzzle table, a desk with a computer that was now smoking, a bullet hole in its monitor, two leather chairs, an end table dripping whiskey and surrounded by shattered glass, and a reading lamp that sparked. A woman was sobbing.

As Taylor got deeper into the room, he saw that it was the same woman who had been cold and rude to him a moment ago. She was leaning over a man who took one bullet to the eye socket and one to the heart. "No, no, no, no," she just kept saying.

Taylor looked around for the shooter. The window nearby was gone. Only shards of broken glass remained. "Did you see them?" he asked.

"Why are you still here? What do you want?" she screamed with fury. "My William is dead, God damn you."

Taylor frowned and looked out the window. He saw someone running in the distance. Grumbling, he climbed through the broken window, trying his best not to skewer himself on a loose shard and he took off after them. They had a huge headstart on him and he couldn't make out any details. After a while, he lost sight of them completely but he followed the sound of their steps. He could still hear them running hard.

Then he couldn't. Taylor ran past green grass and foliage onto a main road and found himself alone. He doubled over and panted for breath as he looked around. He saw no one in any direction, just huge houses and big fences, with seemingly endless miles of property. "Shit," he said. He didn't even know how to get back to the car from here.

Taylor took out his phone and called it in. "We got a homicide out here. Someone shot Lance's father. Well-placed shots. The misses were probably intentional. I chased after the shooter but he had a big headstart and I lost him. I lost everything. I have no idea where I am right now. There's no street sign either. I'll try to find one. Make sure the boys are careful when they're looking for this guy. He's armed and dangerous. There's a lot of damned places to hide unfortunately... Too many."

"Heading your way now, Conroy. Do not engage until we arrive."

"Yeah, I know. I got it."

lll

TAYLOR FUMBLED WITH HIS keys and opened the door, stumbling into a dark apartment, rubbing his eyes as he went. He slipped his shoes off and pushed them to the wall beside the welcome mat. Then he shuffled, exhausted, to the bedroom. Eric was asleep, sprawled out with a book on his chest. The lamp was still on beside the bed and there was a full wine glass and an empty bottle. Taylor sighed. He climbed into bed and wrapped his arm around Eric's midsection. "So much for Indian," Eric mumbled.

"I'm sorry," Taylor whispered. "My witness was killed and the perp was still on the grounds. I had to wait on backup and we searched for hours only to come up empty. I tried to still get food but they were closed. Raincheck?"

Eric was snoring quietly. Taylor sighed again. "We'll talk tomorrow." He kissed his husband's stubble. He snuggled up close and tried to sleep. His brain refused to let him though. The father's death was very different than the son's. Lance was taken apart over time. There was an entire well of rage that went into the way he was shredded and flung about. His father on the other hand had been executed by someone with training. There were some wild shots into the room and two perfectly placed kill shots. It was done quickly and efficiently. In both instances someone clearly wanted to take them out but Taylor had a hard time believing it was the same person. He saw Eric's phone light up on the nightstand and he reached over his sleeping husband to grab it.

A new message had come through.

SAMARA

> Here's the pics you wanted. Hope you can get him to understand.

Taylor looked at the photos and knew without explanation that they were of Gary. It was brutal. The kid's face was a pile of lumps like it was made out of cream of wheat. His eyes were purple orbs, swollen shut with contusions and lacerations that gaped like tiny mouths all over. His lips were shaped all wrong, the bones of his jaw out of alignment. It was hard to tell from the tubes and bandages but it looked like he was missing a lot of teeth as well.

He frowned and put the phone back on Eric's nightstand. He replaced it with the glass of wine and sipped it while he stared at the wall in the dark. He already knew what Eric was going to say to him. "Lance didn't deserve what happened to him but Gary did?"

Neither of them did, Taylor thought. *No one deserves that. No one.*

IV

He'd fallen asleep sitting up, the empty wine glass still in hand. He groaned and struggled out of bed, stiff and sore. After stumbling drunkenly to the kitchen he found Eric by the counter. He poured a cup of coffee and handed it to Taylor, who tried to kiss the man. Eric stopped him with a finger on his lips. "Not til you've brushed those teeth."

"That's fair. I'm really sorry about dinner."

Eric met his eyes with a harshness Taylor was unaccustomed to. "I tried to wait up and couldn't do it anymore. Couldn't you have texted?"

"There was an armed perp lurking about. He was a crack shot. If I let my guard down, he could have killed me. We didn't even catch him."

"Who'd he shoot?"

"Lance's dad, right through the eye and another in the heart."

"Someone killed the piece of shit that harasses us and attacks us and now someone killed the man who made him who he was and you want me to see this as bad."

Taylor put two slices of wheat bread in the toaster and sipped his coffee. "Last I checked, murder was wrong. I had to pass a test on stuff like that to become detective. I definitely got that question right. Murder is wrong."

"Even when it helps the world? Look at these pictures of Gary, Tay. What if that had been me?"

Taylor looked at the pictures even though they were burned into his mind when they came through in the night. "Then I would have made sure he went to prison for what he did."

"Well, the cops who showed up that night didn't." Taylor sipped his coffee as the toaster dinged and the bread popped up, smelling delicious and looking a perfect golden brown. He made a mental note to find out exactly who those cops were.

"That was wrong and those officers should be punished accordingly just like the perpetrator of the crime."

"Oh get off it, Tay. You're not at work. You're home...with me. I'm not asking how the detective feels. I'm asking how the gay man feels."

"Sad. I feel sad, Eric, and tired, so very tired. All of this is exhausting and depressing. A man driven by hate was killed and the father he was for some reason estranged from was also killed and the only eye witness was full of hate, my husband is full of hate. No one seems to realize that it's a vicious cycle that does nothing but poison all of us."

Eric glared at him. "You know who didn't hate? Gary. Look where it got him." He stormed off. Taylor watched him go but didn't move to go after him.

His phone buzzed in his pocket and he pulled it out. "Yeah."

"We found it." Tucci's words were laced with excitement.

"*It?*"

"The knife. You were right. It was a big ass mean looking kitchen knife, Conroy."

"Where?"

"Couple of goons were arrested on drugs. One of them had it in the car, still bloody."

Taylor shook his head. He shrugged his coat on as he buttered his toast. Then he took the toast and the coffee to the door. He stepped into his shoes and looked back at the bedroom. Then he left. "Goons? You're telling me that Lance was a hit?"

"Seems so, buddy. They already tested the blood on the knife. It was a match. Neither one of these guys is talking."

"Something doesn't add up." Taylor placed his coffee on the roof of his car and tugged the driver's side door open. "His father seemed more like a hit. I've never, in twelve years, seen a hit that messy."

"Yeah, you're right. When we tried to grill these punks, their mouths were clamped shut but their eyes burned with hatred, well one more than the other. There was a definite vendetta."

"Alright. I'm gonna swing by the Bird Cage and talk to a few people. Then I'm heading to the station to question those guys myself."

"Good luck."

V

TAYLOR WALKED INTO THE bar. He was getting the stink eye from everyone. He knew they saw him as the bad guy now but he wasn't going to argue. He just frowned and headed to the bar. "Hey, Luke."

"Drinking on the job today?" Luke said with his boyish smile wedged between big dimples.

"I wish. I'm investigating the murder of Lance Kent." He heard the mumbles all around but didn't look at anyone but the man before him.

Luke looked around at the other patrons. He turned to a woman going over glasses with a rag. "Tammy, watch the bar for a minute."

She nodded and he led Taylor to his office in the back. When the door closed, Luke said, "Lance wasn't a bad guy, not really. He was mixed up, you know? Sure, it was fucked what he did to Gary but I don't think that was really about Gary. His parents disowned him and froze his trust fund and all other assets they could. He got in with mob

113

guys to try to make some of that money back. I think he hung out here to get away from them because it was the one bar in town that they didn't own, and regularly visit, but then when he was here his father's voice was in his head, telling him we were going to think he was queer. The whole thing is a mess."

"How do you know all this?"

"Every drunk talks to the bartender, even the homophobic ones. Plus, I'm bi and my girlfriend is straight so she doesn't like to spend all her time at the gay bar. When I go to her bars, there's old Lance and his new pals. Some of those places are fronts and word was Lance was going to move up, get his own gig. I guess that ain't happening."

Taylor exhaled, his shoulders slumping. He patted the other man on the shoulder but Luke came in for a hug, embracing him. "You look like shit," the bartender told him. "Get some sleep."

"I'd love to. As soon as all this is over."

Taylor pulled out his phone on the way to the car. "I got some interesting info. I'm on the way over there."

"Good, cause we got a mess, bud."

"What? Why? What now?"

"You should probably see for yourself."

VI

TAYLOR GOT TO THE precinct and heard the commotion before he came through the doors. "How the hell did this happen?" the captain yelled. "Why wasn't anyone watching?"

Taylor saw Tucci and hurried over to him. "Conroy, hey...follow me."

He led Taylor to an interrogation room. There was blood and skull fragments everywhere. One of the mob guys was on the floor, still in the chair, his head caved in like an overripe fruit that collapsed. "Did it himself," Tucci said. "Smashed the table til there wasn't much left. I'd been the one in here with him and I left to talk to the Captain about strategies since he wouldn't open up. I didn't expect him to do this shit."

"Where's the other guy?"

"Locked up tight. Sanchez is watching him like a hawk. Guess he knew with the mess he made he was going away for a long time."

"Maybe." Taylor chewed on his lip as he went to go find the surviving killer. When he did, the man was sitting in a cell glaring at him like he had been the one to kill the man's friend. Taylor patted Sanchez on the back.

"Hell of a mess we got, ain't it?" Sanchez said.

Taylor looked at the man through the bars. "What would make your buddy kill himself so violently like that?"

"Violence is kinda his thing, but you knew that already didn't you? He didn't have a good role model growing up or whatever *Law and Order* blames that shit on."

Taylor refused to take the bait. "What about you? Violence your thing?"

The man said nothing. He just stared forward smugly. "You ain't getting anything out of these guys," Sanchez said. "They ever figure out who was putting the flowers and rainbows and shit in your locker?"

"Nope. Hey, there was an incident last month at the Bird Cage. Kid got beaten bad, permanently disfigured. You know who answered that call?"

"First I'm hearing of it."

Taylor huffed. "That's a bad sign. Okay, stay vigilant. I'm gonna go visit our dead goon's house, see if it won't talk more than he did."

"You won't find anything there," the guy said from his cell.

"Says the guy who was driving around with a bloodstained murder weapon." Taylor headed back to the front for the info on who the dead mobster was.

When he had what he was looking for he headed back to the car. After a stop at a drive thru for a fresh cup of joe, he made his way to townhouse where Enrico Mangioni and his brother lived. He stared at the front door before getting out of the car. "What made you so enraged, Enrico? What made you scatter Lance like that?"

He got out and caught the harsh stares. Taylor flashed his badge at them as he made his way by. He went to Enrico's door and opened it with the key that had been in his pocket when he died. Taylor looked over his shoulder to ensure no one was going to take a shot at him. Then he went in and closed the door. His mouth fell open. The walls were covered with canvases all painted with aggression and passion, colors sprayed and splattered across their expanse.

"You looking for my brother?" a voice said, drawing Taylor's gaze away from the artwork. There was a teenage boy in the hall looking at him. "He ain't here and I don't know when he's gonna be back."

"He's not coming back, kid," Taylor said, his voice thick with remorse. He showed his badge. "I'm sorry. He was arrested for something and he took his own life."

The boy shook his head. "Nah. He wouldn't do that. He was going to have his first gallery soon. Enrico was gonna go big time."

Taylor frowned. "I'm really sorry. What do you know about Lance Kent?"

The boy's eyes narrowed and blazed with anger. "Was this because of him? Anzeloni was right. He said Lance was gonna ruin everything, that Enrico was gonna end up in prison instead of an art gallery because of that asshole. They never should have let him in."

"Why? Why was he a danger to your brother?"

"Fuckin guy was running with my brother, acting like they were best buds, family even, and then it turns out the son of a bitch was dating a cop on the DL."

Taylor tried not to let his shock show. That would explain why he was driven home instead of arrested on the night with Gary. Was the cop that picked him up his partner? "You don't know the cop's name do you?"

"Nah. Enrico wouldn't tell me. He said he wanted to keep me clean so he never told me shit. Anything I knew I heard from the other guys."

"Alright. Thanks. You've been a big help. I'm sorry again about your brother."

The boy fought back tears and nodded.

When Taylor made it back to his car. He sat behind the wheel for a minute with his face buried in his hands. This case was getting more horrific instead of better. Everyone was doing horrible things because they thought they were doing right. They were all just trying to live. He felt like he needed a vacation.

Taylor drove back to the Bird Cage. When he went in, he said, "Luke, I need your help with something else."

"Get the hell out of here," someone yelled, throwing a beer mug at him. It crashed into the bar and shattered.

"Alright. Out!" Luke shouted at them, pointing.

"You're not welcome in here anymore," a woman snapped before spitting at Taylor.

"Maybe we can talk in your office again?" Taylor asked.

"Tammy?"

"Got it," she said without looking up from what she was doing. Luke led Taylor to the back.

"I'm really sorry about that. Tensions are high right now."

"I get it. I'm gonna show you some pictures from my phone. I need you to tell me if any of the people in them was the officer that came here the night Gary got beaten."

When Luke nodded, Taylor showed him the phone. "Just swipe right."

"I don't need to. That's him right there."

Taylor looked at the photo and Luke pointed again. "Holy shit," Taylor said out loud. "Thanks, Luke. I gotta go."

Taylor rushed out through the bar with more things being thrown as the patrons heckled him. He got to the car in a hurry and raced away.

VII

TAYLOR RUSHED INTO THE police station. He found Tucci, grabbed him by the arm and dragged him into a nearby interrogation room. "You didn't think to mention you were dating Lance Kent?"

Tucci's eyes fluttered around. He looked at the two-way mirror and the cameras. "Keep it down alright. I don't want the other guys to know I'm... You know... Like that."

"For god's sake, man. You can't even say gay?"

"I'm not. I mean, not completely. I go out with girls too or I did before Lance."

"Did you kill Enrico?"

"I was with the captain. He did it himself."

"You had something to do with it. I know you did. Start talking."

"Alright. Settle down okay? Listen. I told him to do it. I said he had five minutes to get it done or I was gonna go put a bullet in his brother's head. He took me seriously."

"Jesus, Tucci."

"Hey, it was an empty threat. I didn't actually do anything to the guy but he deserved to fucking die, Conroy. He took away my uh.... The um... I loved that guy, okay?"

Taylor rubbed at his face. "I'm so sick of everyone thinking everyone else deserves to die. No one has the right to decide that. What about Lance's dad? Did you do that? Was it you I chased all over creation and disappointed my husband for?"

Tucci's eye burned with hatred. "It was all that bastard's fault. He found out about me and Lance and disowned him, took all his money. It's because of him that Lance ended up with those assholes and got killed. He never would have had to do that if his father could have just loved him for who he was."

And he wouldn't have done what he did to Gary if he could have loved himself for who he was, Taylor thought. "This is a damned mess."

"You can't turn me in, Conroy. I mean, don't you understand? You're gay."

Taylor felt a surge of anger but he closed his eyes and took a deep breath. When he exhaled he reopened his eyes. "I'm sorry," he said.

Taylor opened the door and walked to the captain. As he began to fill him in, a gunshot sounded behind them. "Fuck."

Taylor just hung his head as the captain ran past him to see what had happened. This time Taylor took out his phone. He texted Eric.

ME

I don't know if I can do this anymore.

"Tucci's dead," someone shouted.

122

Taylor found a nearby chair and all but fell into it. His phone buzzed and he looked at it through the tears welling up in his eyes.

Eric

> Me neither. I'm leaving. I'll be gone by the time you get home.

"Not what I meant," Taylor said, but didn't bother texting back. He threw his phone in a nearby wastebasket. Then he leaned his head back and moaned, quietly voicing the pain in his heart.

Taylor could hear cops shouting about Tucci. He could hear the other perp yelling from holding, "Was that him? Was that the guy Lance was blabbing to? Serves him right. He had it coming."

"Shut up," Sanchez shouted. "Shut the hell up or you're gonna have it coming."

Taylor got to his feet. He wiped his wet eyes with the backs of his hands. Then he headed into the captain's office. He laid his gun and his badge on the desk and wrote on a nearby pad of post-it notes. "I'm done. Sorry. Tay—"

Then he walked out of the building. Even in the open air of the outside, it felt suffocating. It was everywhere. Hatred. Anger. The justification of death. It was coming from all sides. He couldn't breathe. He tugged at his collar on the way to his car. When he got in and closed the door, he didn't even start the engine. He shook and broke into sobs, clawing at his shirt. He reached to the floorboard as his chest tightened more and the car felt like it was bending towards him, crushing him. He grabbed an old fast food paper bag and held it to his face. Taylor breathed into the bag until he calmed down. Then with his still trembling fingers he started the engine. He pulled away from the curb and drove to the highway. He didn't know where he was going. He just needed to get away, but he knew deep down there was no real escape. It was everywhere.

This is the world we live in now.

SKELETONS

1

J OHN SCRATCHED AT HIS stubble. *It's way too early for this shit.*
He got out of the car and groaned when his back popped. *And I'm
too damn old for it.* He went to take a sip of coffee and the lid wasn't
on tightly. Coffee spilled onto his white button-down shirt leaving it
spotted with what looked like pools of mud. "Fantastic," he grumbled.
"Son of a bitch."

He took out a cigarette and had a coughing fit before he could get
it lit. "Damn it to hell." He coughed. *This damn job is gonna be the
death of me.*

He lit the cigarette, took a drag, and fixed the lid on his coffee.
After a sip, he walked up to the warehouse. He got to the caution tape
and flashed his badge, almost dropping his whole cup of coffee in the
process and cursing under his breath.

"Bout time, Fratelli," his partner said, walking over as John ducked
under the tape. "As lead detective, you think you'd be punctual."

"Fuck off, Murphy. It's 4 a.m. I'm fat and old. Cut me some slack."

Murphy looked at the cigarette in John's hand. "Where do you even find those things anymore? Everyone vapes these days, Fratelli."

"I'm not doing that shit. I don't want to smoke a damned sugar cookie like the woke kids. You gonna fill me in on what's going on or not?"

Murphy sighed. He started walking into the warehouse and John tried to keep up without spilling his coffee. "Place has been out of business, abandoned for a long time. Some punk kids, and I don't mean that as an insult—I mean they were literally punks—like denim jackets with anarchy symbols and mohawks and the whole nine, had broken in to make out. They found the body by accident and called it in."

"Good. Arrest them for trespassing. Then we can have 'em around for any more questions we might have."

"Seriously? Jesus, Fratelli, they're kids. You didn't break into abandoned places when you were a kid?"

"Doesn't make it less of a crime. I was smart enough not to get caught."

"They got caught because they called us. For god's sake, man. You'll just teach the youth to cover their asses and *not* call us when shit like this happens."

"Every time you open your mouth, you remind me of why I don't like you. Probably drink Bud Light."

"For real? I'm a craft beer, IPA guy actually, you damn curmudgeon. Body is this way."

"That's not better," John said as he followed him. He coughed and took another drag off his cigarette. "You probably listen to that Taylor Swift."

"Is that supposed to be an insult?" Eoin Murphy said with a laugh. "Taylor Swift is a musical genius."

John mumbled something under his breath and continued, "I need to retire."

"No argument there." Murphy pointed forward.

"In the closet? I didn't think anyone was in the closet these days."

"Too soon, Fratelli. Jesus."

"What? Everyone and their brother is some kind of Morse code semicolon sexual or some shit. I don't even know anymore." John shrugged his big shoulders and walked to the closet door. He peeked inside and immediately turned away. "Christ. Good thing I didn't have breakfast. How the fuck long has this guy been in there? It is a guy, right? I don't want to get canceled or whatever."

Eoin shook his head. "Fratelli, no one knows you or cares or you would have been canceled years ago. Forensics said several days, a week maybe."

"Damn guy is a mess. I thought people could go a month without food."

"Not without water, Fratelli. Closet was locked. Heat was on. Our guy ran out of sweat. Died of dehydration. Brain swelling, kidney failure, ugly stuff. We won't know for sure until the toxicology report comes back but it looks and smells like he was given something to make him vomit and have diarrhea. That would speed up the dehydration process. Guy could have been dead in a couple of days."

"Is it him?" another voice asked. Both men turned.

"Hey, Paulie," Eoin said. "There was no ID on the body and he's in bad shape but you can take a look."

"The hell you can," John said, blocking his path. "This is an active crime scene. You shouldn't even be here."

Paulie smirked at him. "Says the guy who was smoking and dribbling coffee everywhere. Nice shirt, by the way. Where did you drop that butt also?"

"Hell outta here, Paisano. I don't want a P.I. at my crime scene," John snapped.

"A P.I. or a queer?" Paulie shot back.

"Both."

"Alright. Enough," Eoin said. "Paulie's here because I called him. He's been tracking a missing person for days. Captain Marlowe thought it might be him. So just let him look, and stay out of his way."

John stared into Paulie's eyes. He pointed at the man's face. "You look, but don't touch a goddamned thing."

"Got it." Paulie eased past him and looked into the closet. He cringed and crinkled his nose. He put a hand to his mouth and turned back to them. "Crap. It's him. That means he's probably been in this closet the whole time I've been looking for him. I gotta go break it to his husband."

"Husband?" John said. "This guy was a—"

"Don't." Paulie jabbed a finger at him. "Just don't."

"Gay, a gay. It's kind of important, no? Someone put a gay in a closet. How much do you know about this guy, Paisano? Any idea when he came out of the closet? Who it was to?"

"Oh, now you want my help?" Paulie said with a humorless laugh.

"No. I don't want anything to do with you people. I *need* your help. There's a difference."

Paulie looked at Eoin. "Did this fuckin' guy just 'you people' me?"

"Yeah, he's a dick, but he's right we could use your help. It's not for Fratelli. It's for the guy you've spent the week looking for."

Paulie huffed. "I don't know the answers to those questions, but I can find out. Give me the day. I'll call you."

"Don't you ever get tired of being a grumpy old bigot?" Eoin said when Paulie walked away.

"That guy had to walk away from the force cause he cheated on his wife with his male partner and *I'm* the problem? Unbelievable." John shook his head.

"He's a good detective, Fratelli. That should be all that matters."

John grumbled. He looked at the dead man's dried-out eyes staring up at him. His eyes moved to the door that was covered in scratches, and he sighed. *What a mess. What a damned mess.*

2

TAYLOR ANSWERED HIS PHONE. When he heard Paulie's voice on the other end he felt equal parts excited and afraid. "What do you got for me?"

"Your instincts were right," Paulie told him. "I found Jack's husband today. It isn't pretty. Brings up more questions than answers."

"Shit," Taylor said. "I knew it. I goddamned knew it. You want to tell Jack or you want me to do it?"

"I'll do it. I'm gonna have to ask him some questions."

"Why would you have to ask him questions, Paulie? I hired you. Your job is done. You're not a cop anymore."

"I told them I would help even though the detective running the case is an old prick that probably used to beat up gay kids in high school."

"Why? Why even get involved?"

"You're the one who got me involved, Tay. You knew something was wrong. Why don't you meet me for breakfast? We can talk more."

"Yeah, alright, but it's not like a date or anything."

Paulie laughed. "Of course not, not yet anyway."

"That's a bit cocky of you."

"I'm a bit cocky."

"And a bit typical. Meet me at the diner on Fifth."

"See you in thirty."

***

Taylor walked into the diner rubbing his eyes. He definitely needed another cup of coffee, but at least he was in the right place for it. He saw Paulie straight away and walked over to sit on the other side of his booth. The server came over and Taylor ordered a coffee, black, and some eggs and bacon. Paulie ordered a Reuben and said, "What? I don't like breakfast food."

Taylor shrugged and laughed at him. "So talk to me," he said.

"So, Jack and David were married, yeah?"

"I mean, not officially, not yet anyway, but we all knew they would be. They definitely acted married."

"I see."

"What do you see?"

"How long would you say David was out of the closet?"

"I don't know. Why? I mean, I've personally known them for just a few months but it seemed to me like they'd been together for years."

Paulie nodded. He thanked the server who came to top off his coffee. "So it is possible that their relationship began when he was in the closet, maybe even married to a woman?"

"What are you getting at, Paulie? You think he was killed out of jealousy or revenge? Keep in mind, I used to be a detective too."

"I don't know yet, and I do know that, but I also know you quit because it was destroying you, and I don't want to bring you too deep into something that could drag you to a dark place."

Taylor eyed him with a strange sense of curiosity. "Alright, now you've intrigued me, not about the case, but about you. You've come across as a typical gay man to me, but I barely know you and that was really empathetic and compassionate."

"Actually I'm bi and were you just insinuating that gay men are not empathetic or compassionate?"

Taylor gave an awkward laugh. "I'm just saying I've encountered a lot of narcissism and my own husband left me because I was trying to solve a case, because it was my job, and the victim was a guy like the detective you're dealing with now."

"Wow."

"I dated this guy named Chadwick once. He was so full of himself, I think he may have even been a serial killer. One time I slipped when I was going down on him. I smacked my nose on his pelvic bone and bled. This guy was so upset that I got a single drop of blood on his bedspread that he dumped me right there in the moment. Threw me out on my ass, bleeding."

Paulie laughed. He stopped to thank the server who was delivering their food. "Maybe you dodged a bullet. Say the guy really was a killer but you freaked him out and that's why you lived."

Taylor laughed as well. "I thought about that but then I thought, if the guy got that freaked out about a single drop of blood, there's no way he could be a killer. He was weird though. Kept fixating on my eyes, like really fixating, like he wanted them on his mantle or something. Yeesh." He shivered and hugged himself.

They took a few minutes to dig into their food and enjoy the meal without talking. Then Paulie broke the silence by saying, "David was in a closet, Tay." Taylor was still chewing but he locked eyes with the man across from him. Paulie nodded. "For the whole time I was looking, like he'd been put there day one, locked in. He died of dehydration."

"Jesus."

"Yeah, it was ugly. I just need to figure out if the closet was a coincidence or symbolism."

"Damn it man, this is exactly what I walked away from."

"Well, you quitting doesn't make the world a better, more accepting place, Tay. It just means it's not your job to arrest the scumbags."

"Yeah, I guess. I do wish I could live somewhere where the truth wasn't so out in the open. Maybe I need to go maroon myself on an island or something."

"I think that's about what it would take. So you in?"

"In? In what? No. I'm not in anything. I was worried about a friend. That's as far as my involvement goes."

Paulie nodded. "Alright then. So you don't want me to tell you what I find?"

"Come on. Of course, I do. I just don't want to find it with you."

"Fair enough. Good Reuben."

3

LOOKING AT THE LAVENDER house, Paulie frowned. He hated making these kinds of visits when he was on the force and he hated them still. Sighing, he made his way up the curving cobblestone walkway, noting how nice the garden was when he passed. He climbed the three stone steps and knocked on the door. It was only a moment before it opened and Jack stood before him with bloodshot eyes. The guy looked like he hadn't slept since David went missing. Paulie nodded and did his best to smile.

"Hi. I'm Paulie Paisano, a private detective. Your friend Taylor hired me to look for your husband, David. May I come in?"

Jack swallowed and nodded. "Yes, of course, come in. Taylor is wonderful. I can't believe he did that. Police don't care too much for people like us."

"Some of them do," Paulie said. "There's a lot of good people on the force. There's good and bad just like there is with any other profession."

"I guess," Jack said, closing the door behind him. "I was just making tea. Would you like some tea?"

"That actually sounds wonderful." He followed Jack to the kitchen where he poured two cups of tea. "Honey if you got it."

"Of course I have it. You know he's not technically my husband. I mean, we planned to make it official, but now I don't know if we'll get the chance."

Paulie wasn't ready to answer that for him yet. "Where should we sit to talk," he said instead.

"Let's go out on the back deck. It's better out there, peaceful. There's a koi pond. It was David's idea."

"Sounds wonderful."

They went outside and sat at a finished wood table with an umbrella. Paulie looked at the koi fish swimming in the pond below and thought how much his wife would have liked them. He tried to contain the frown that wanted to happen. "So if you weren't married but friends like Taylor saw you as married, how long were you and David together if you don't mind me asking?"

Jack looked embarrassed by the question. He sipped his tea and looked out at the trees that stood like guardians past the edges of the perfectly manicured lawn.

Paulie understood how he felt. "I was a detective for the police but I slept with my partner when I was married. Screwed up my career and my marriage."

"Why are you telling me this?"

"My male partner."

"Oh."

"So, you and David... How long?"

Jack sighed. "A long time. Jesus, as long as I can remember really. We were best friends since we were kids, but David's family didn't like queers. He played the part forever. It killed me to be his dark secret instead of his sunshine and happiness. I told him that a few months ago. I said I would call it quits and find someone who was able to be what I deserved. We both cried and then he did it. I couldn't believe it. He actually did it. He left his wife. He was disowned by his parents. He hadn't spoken to his extended family at all. He gave it all up for me. For me. Then not three months later, he disappears. I'm afraid it was just too much; the weight was too heavy. I'm afraid he ran away or worse, hurt himself."

Paulie exhaled and rubbed the tension from his face. He considered not saying anything about David's body yet, but now he felt like he had to. He took a deep breath and focused on the fish when he said, "He didn't kill himself."

Jack jumped like he'd seen a ghost. "You know? You found him? Where is he? What happened? Tell me. Please. I have to know."

Fuck. This sucks. This really fucking sucks. Paulie huffed. "Someone hurt him, Jack. I'm sorry. He is gone. I'm so sorry."

There was a moment of silence and stillness. Then Jack started to shake. The chair moved and he collapsed to the floor. "Shit," Paulie said quietly.

He got down on the ground and gathered the man up in his arms, holding him tightly while he spasmed, seized, screamed, and sobbed. "I'm so sorry," he repeated, feeling genuine emotion for this man he'd never met before today.

Paulie didn't want to ask anything else until Jack had gotten it out and grown calm. He deserved these minutes to feel his pain. He just sat there on the deck and held him, until his sobs quieted. "Do you know anyone who would have hurt him?" His voice was solemn. "Did his father hate queers that much?"

Jack shook his head. "No, he was an asshole for sure but he was still his dad. He loved him. He wouldn't do that. I can't imagine anyone would do that. You have never met anyone as sweet as that man, I promise you. How could anyone hurt him, take him from this earth? It's wrong, it's just wrong."

Paulie nodded even though the man in his arms couldn't see it. "It is, and I promise you, I'm gonna find him. That's why I need to talk to you, to ask you some questions to get information that could help."

Jack nodded. He worked to stand. When they both took their seats, Jack's expression was hard, focused, and angry. "What do you need to know?" he said, his voice monotone like a robot, but with an edge that could be heard if you were listening close enough.

Paulie reached across the table and put a hand over Jack's. "Everything," he said. "Tell me everything."

4

TAYLOR WAS PACING. HE couldn't handle seeing the gory details of how much the world hated the LGBTQI+ community. It was overwhelming, crazy-making. But quitting his job didn't fix anything. You didn't have to be a homicide detective to see what atrocities were committed upon people just for being who they were and loving who they loved. You just had to be alive. It didn't matter where you went either. Hatred was everywhere. He felt like he could move to Mars and there would be some kind of homophobic aliens living in the rock.

Bang!

He could still hear the gunshot. Another man on the force took his own life right there at the precinct because the case Taylor was working would have dragged him out of the closet. For him, being dead was better than being queer. Moving to a different place couldn't erase the sound of the gunshot from Taylor's mind. It lived there rent-free and would forever.

He wanted to be free, to just...be, but it felt unrealistic. What if he could help find who killed David, if he could stop more people like himself from being hurt just for existing in the world with someone who saw them as an abomination? Shouldn't he?

He couldn't help but wonder what it would do to him though, to go down this rabbit hole. Taylor had always believed in the system. He believed in the law. He cared only about innocent and guilty and being a good cop. It cost him his marriage, took another cop's life, and left him broken. Part of him really did understand why the bullied fought back, why the abused hurt their abusers. If he kept going, Taylor didn't know when he would cross that line, when he would go from being someone who believed in the system to someone who just wanted to kill the prick who did this.

If he made that leap, Taylor would no longer be who he wanted to be anymore. He became a cop because he wanted to make the world better, not to become a monster like everyone else. At the same time, he didn't know if he was physically able to turn a blind eye to this. That might eat at him just as badly. He felt so lost. He didn't even have a destination anymore. His stomach twisted in knots.

Taylor huffed. He walked over to his small two-person table in his quaint one-bedroom apartment, and he seized the bottle of whiskey that sat in its center beside a vase of fake flowers. He scoffed at the image. He got the fake flowers so they wouldn't die, so there would be some goodness that always remained but now he was seeing it differently. Just like all the goodness he tried to focus on, the flowers were fake. The beauty wasn't real. It was an illusion, something he created to make himself feel better. He sometimes wondered if that's what his marriage was.

Fuck. He opened the whiskey and turned it up, groaning and grimacing at the harshness of it but ultimately relaxing when the burn hit his chest. When he put the bottle down, he made a decision. If he could help, he had to. If it destroyed him, it would have to. There was no running away from this, not this time, but when it was over, he was going to be done. He would find that island, and avoid relationships to avoid the hate. He would live alone in the safety of his bubble like the fake flower he was.

Sighing, he took out his phone and called Paulie Paisano. When he heard the gruff "Hello," Taylor frowned. The man sounded exhausted, not just physically but mentally and emotionally. It was something Taylor understood well. When he hadn't said anything, Paulie spoke again. "If you got something, Tay, hit me with it. It's a rough night."

Taylor cleared his throat. "Sorry. I just... I wanted to say I was in, that I'll help you find David's killer."

"Well, it's perfect timing but you may regret that decision," Paulie told him.

"Why?"

"Because I just got off the phone with John Fratelli's much more reasonable partner. He's an ally in more ways than one."

"And?"

"And there's been another one, Tay."

"Another one?"

"Seems this wasn't someone with a personal grudge against David after all. Looks like we got a serial bigot on our hands."

Taylor sighed. "Can I recant my offer?"

"That's up to you, but make it quick. I'm heading over there before Fratelli spills coffee all over the crime scene."

143

"That guy won't let me anywhere near it. I'm not a cop anymore or a P.I. like you."

"Sure you are. You're my partner. How funny would it be to be the PC detective agency? Paisano and Conroy of course but that's good comedy."

"Except I'm not licensed."

"Yet. Let me worry about that. Let me worry about Fratelli too. Eoin knows me. He won't let the old grump push me out."

Taylor thought for a moment, and then said, "Alright. Give me the address."

"Attaboy."

"I'm not agreeing to the PC agency. I want this to be the last case for the rest of my life."

"Mmhmm. We'll see about that. You got it in your blood whether you like it or not, Tay. Some people can walk away and detach from it and then there's people like us, proof being that you called me in the first place. Even if your mind says let it go, your instincts aren't going to just shut off and your heart isn't going to change. We are who we are."

Taylor huffed. "Address."

5

E OIN WAS THE FIRST at the scene. He walked up to the house. It looked like something out of a scary movie, tall and weathered, dark with broken shutters that hung like useless limbs. There were 2x4s on the windows and a sheet of plywood nailed where one had been clearly broken. The stone steps that led to the front door were chipped and broken. He thought back to being a kid, skipping around on the concrete because stepping on a crack broke your mother's back. His mother had it hard enough. She was a nurse, working long hours and lacking appreciation for it.

Two uniformed officers met him at the edge of the property. The one on the left, Ringold, said, "Kids again. Broke in through the back to smash and discovered our guy. They're pretty shaken up. As soon as they told us we called you."

"I appreciate it. Closet?"

The other officer nodded. He was a rookie, a young kid named Turner. "Ugly scene. You think our killer is a Trumper?"

"I think we should definitely not bring politics into something like this without evidence. This isn't social media. It's a crime scene."

"Right. Sorry." Turner frowned.

"You boys call a bus to take care of those kids?"

"Yes, sir. It's on the way."

"Good. Show me to them. Then keep everyone else out except the people that are supposed to be here. I have P.I. help on this one. When he gets here, he'll show you ID. Let him in."

"You got it," Ringold said. Turner gave a shy smile, obviously still feeling embarrassed, and led the detective around to the back of the house. The kids were sitting on the back porch wrapped in a dark blue police-issued blanket and hugging each other. "Keaton and Louis."

Eoin frowned. *Gay kids. Hope that bus gets here fast. John will eat these kids alive.*

He walked up to them. "Hey," he said, trying his best to give a reassuring smile, though he wasn't sure it was worth much. "I'm Detective Murphy." He showed them his badge to ease their nerves. Poor kids looked terrified. "What happened here tonight?"

"Louis's dad is a prick. Threw us out. We knew this place was abandoned so we thought it would be safe. We never expected…"

"Alright. It's okay. You really are safe now. I just need all the details you can give me."

"We heard something," Louis said. "Could have been a rat or something but we got nervous. We thought it could have been my dad, like maybe he followed us or something."

Keaton jumped in. "Or it could have been skinheads. We know they hand out in abandoned places and there's some disturbing graffiti in there."

"If we could break in, someone else could too, and maybe they would hate us like my dad and want to hurt us."

"We went to hide in the closet."

"It was locked but we were really scared so I used the crowbar I used to break in."

"That's when we saw the woman and freaked out."

Eoin's mind was reeling. A woman this time. He was expecting a man. They heard someone in there with them. Could it have been the killer? "How long ago was this?"

Keaton shook his head. "I don't know. Maybe ten minutes?"

Eoin looked at Ringold. "Did you or Turner see anyone come out of that house?"

The officer shook his head. "I didn't. I suppose they could have snuck out when we were taking care of the kids, but no, I didn't see anyone."

"Dammit." Eoin drew his gun. He looked at the uniformed officer. "Be on guard. Watch these kids. Do what I said and tape this place off. Anyone but me comes out of that house, tackle the shit out of them."

Ringold nodded but he looked nervous. Eoin looked back at the road wondering where his partner was. Then he bounded up the steps past the frightened children and into the house. He immediately drew his flashlight and held it with his gun in a cross pattern out in front of him. The place was incredibly dark. He flicked a light switch. Nothing happened. Power was probably shut off long ago but he had to try. If that guy was in here somewhere he didn't want him to get the jump on him. Plus, the kids were right. His serial killer was not the only dangerous person in this city. Most of the usual vermin were not fond of cops and would attack him just as quickly.

He moved through the dark house, boards creaking under his feet, shining his flashlight everywhere. He kept his ears open for sounds of movement, scuffling, creaking that belonged to feet that weren't his, breathing, anything.

He went room to room moving his flashlight all about, tracing the beam over everything he could. He didn't want to miss a single detail. *Are you in here? Where the hell are you?*

He completed all of the first floor without sight or sound of humans or rodents and made his way to the spiral staircase and its rainbow banister. It made him wonder what this place was. As he ascended his heart was pounding. When he got to the top he saw a hallway decorated with clowns, balloons, and bears. He pushed open the first door and saw a small blackboard on a stand with magnetic letters scattered all around it. There were bright-colored bean bag chairs and a bookcase full of children's books. He swept in quickly and pulled the closet open. The dead woman was staring at him like he was the one who put her in there. Eoin frowned but he couldn't give her the time, not yet.

Eoin quickly backed away and hurried out of the room. He checked the rest of the floor as he didn't see any basement access downstairs. If the killer was still in the house, he had to be up here. There was a bathroom with two sets of plastic steps to help children gain access to the sink and toilet. *Whoever owns this place must have run a daycare up here or something. The downstairs seemed like an ordinary living space but up here is something else.*

He entered the last room at the end of the hall and found himself in a playroom. There were every manner of children's toys scattered in piles all over the room. At the back of the room was a hatch in the slanted ceiling that was either a crawl space or an attic of some kind. Eoin stepped over the plastic dolls and tricycles, broken robots, and the like as he worked his way across the cluttered room. He tripped over a dollhouse, kicking it with his foot and he cursed, looking down at it. His nerves were on edge.

He finally reached the door and he reached up to pull the handle. It came open with a rain of dust and debris and he was left coughing into his elbow. He looked into the darkness and saw the whites of two eyes staring back at him. "I've got you," he said. "I'm gonna back up and I want you to come out slowly. No sudden movements, and keep your hands where I can see them. Now."

Eoin heard Fratelli call his name from downstairs and he looked that way. "Up here!" he called.

When he turned back, he couldn't see the eyes anymore. The perp hadn't obeyed his commands. He or she must have gone deeper into the attic and chose to hide like there was anywhere to go. Why couldn't people ever be sensible and just give themselves up?

Eoin approached the space. There was no ladder to get in. He would have to pull himself up. It was too risky. He would have to wait for Fratelli for that. Still, he stepped closer and shined his flashlight into the darkness beyond the opened trap door to see if he could see where they went. Before he could say anything, a foot kicked his flashlight up into his face. Eoin's gun went off and wood and plaster rained down. He tried to jump back to regain his bearings but the unseen assailant grabbed his collar and pulled him up into the crawlspace. His feet came off the ground. Eoin tried to turn his gun so he could get a shot off but something heavy came down on his head and the world went black.

6

J OHN HEARD THE GUNSHOT and forced his sore, tired old body to move faster, drawing his own gun as he moved through the house. He stubbed his toe and yelled a curse. He hurried up the stairs and went room by room calling for Murphy as he went. When he found him, the detective was face down in a pile of toys. "What the fuck are you doing?" John growled.

He walked towards his partner and nudged him with his foot. "There's a body in this house for god's sake and you're in here taking a nap with the dolls?"

Eoin groaned and put a hand to the back of his head. He rolled, arching his back and grimacing. He'd hit that dollhouse on the way down with his spine. It didn't feel good. "You're a dick," he said. "Did you get him?"

"Who?"

"The guy? The fucking guy was in here, Fratelli. He hit me over the head."

"I didn't see any guy, just you unless you count that Ken doll over there."

"If he didn't go past you, he's gotta still be in here somewhere." Eoin tried to jump up but swayed and almost fell. He stumbled through some toys and braced himself on the wall. "You're a mess," John said. "Stay here. I'll look. The goddamn house creaks like it's dying so it shouldn't be hard to find him if he's here."

"That's what I thought too. Just be careful."

John shook his head and grunted. He hurried out of the room. He went back over the floor he was on, checking the nooks and crannies with his flashlight. He was grumbling curse words the whole way. When he found nothing but a mess that made him glad his kids were grown and out of his hair, John made his way back downstairs. Before checking any of the rooms he checked the front door. It was still locked solidly. He went to the back door, poked his head out, and looked at the new kid, Turner. "Kid...you see anyone come out this door?"

"No, sir."

"Were you looking?"

"Yes, sir."

John grunted and ducked back inside. "Alright, you fucker," he said loudly. "You got no way out of here. Either you're gonna come out and leave in handcuffs or you're gonna do something stupid and leave in a body bag. Your choice."

He waited a bit and just listened. He saw nor heard anything. Whoever the perp was, they were as good at being quiet as they were at hiding. It was pissing John off. "Why hide and go seek huh? How 'bout red light, green light? Or tag? I could get behind those games."

Annoyed, he started to explore. *If he runs out, that kid better do his damn job and stop him. This is already a mess. Too many people have walked and fallen over this crime scene and touched every goddamned thing.*

John went into the downstairs bathroom and tugged the shower curtain back. There was nothing but a tub that desperately needed some Comet. He ducked back out and moved about the living room looking for someplace the guy could hide. There wasn't much. He used his thick fingers to tug open the entertainment center. It had been cleaned out except for webs and spiders.

"When I do get a hold of you, I'm gonna kick your ass just for shits and giggles because you made me hunt for you."

John left and went to the bedroom. He checked under the bed and didn't see anyone hiding down there. It just made him angrier that he was forced to get down and get up. His big body no longer enjoyed those feats. With a groan, he pushed himself up off of the floor, one hand on his lower back. He cursed as he hobbled over and ripped the sliding door closet open. It was as empty as the entertainment center and he cursed again. *Fucker has to be here somewhere.*

John headed back out of the bedroom, twisting and turning to loosen his stiff muscles as he went. "Isn't it usually closeted gay guys that commit violence against other gays? You queer? Huh? Is that why you're mad?"

John walked into the kitchen. He tugged up the pantry doors and stepped back ready to fire his gun if need be. No one rushed out so he peeked inside. There was nothing but empty shelves and a lone dusty single-serve bag of Cheez-Its.

Before John could even curse about it, the cabinet under the sink burst open and a figure dressed in all black with a hood burst out, sprinting for the living room.

"Mother fucker!" John yelled. He forced his big old body to give chase. When he reached the living room, the person was jumping straight for the window beside the front door. John raised his gun and fired. The runner hit the sheet of plywood and went right through it with a crash onto the front porch. John hurried across the room to the now open window. He was hoping he hit the guy. If he did, adrenaline had kicked in because whoever they were jumped up quickly and ran for the street. That goddamned queer detective was out there. John didn't know what he was doing there but he yelled to him. "For fuck's sake, stop him! Get that mother fucker!"

7

P AULIE HAD JUST GOTTEN to the scene. He hadn't seen Taylor yet and was hoping Fratelli didn't cause too big of a fuss. He was still thrown by the fact that there was a second body. His last case as a Long Island police detective was a serial killer. Paulie solved it but a lot of people died in the process. Since he moved and became a P.I., he's kept it simple, finding missing people, and ironically cheating spouses. Sometimes it got ugly for sure, but never serial killer ugly.

Not two steps out of the car, someone in all black wearing a hood came crashing out a boarded-up window of the house and was sprinting for the road. "Shit," Paulie said as he went for his gun.

Fratelli was at the window yelling to him. "Stop him!"

Paulie raised his gun but hadn't fired at anyone since leaving the force. He lowered it and took off at a run behind the person fleeing the crime scene. "Stop!" he called as he gave chase. "Do not make me shoot you."

Whoever they were, (*could it be him?*), they weren't deterred by his threats. They were fast as hell. It took everything Paulie had just to keep close enough to keep them in his line of sight. Paulie was winded, panting, and turning red as he tried to force his body to keep up. This was a sign to him that he wasn't doing enough cardio, not that he was his own boss. "Stop, dammit!"

Taylor's car came flying from a side street and ran right into the guy Paulie was chasing. He slammed on the brakes with a screech and the hooded character rolled up the front of the car, then back down and off of it. He immediately bounded to his feet and took off running again. Paulie snarled and hurried to catch up, raising his gun but lowering it when he saw he was too far for a good shot.

Taylor yelled from the open driver's side window of the car. "Get in! Hurry!"

Panting and gasping, Paulie rounded the car and jumped in the passenger side. "Go! Go!"

The car launched forward. It went all of one block before Taylor slammed on the brakes. The person they were chasing was nowhere to be seen. "Fuck. Did you see which way he went?" Taylor asked.

"I wasn't close enough," Paulie told him. "Took too damn long for me to get there. You should have gone after him without me."

"I'd be up shit's creek if I did. I'm not a cop or a detective, no matter how much you want me to be. I'm just the guy that just hit someone with my car near a crime scene."

"Fuck," Paulie snapped, punching the dash. The glove box popped open and he aggressively slammed it back shut just for it to pop open again. "Damn it!"

"Call it in before he gets too far," Taylor said, bringing him back to the moment.

Paulie nodded. He called Eoin. "Hey, it's Paisano. I chased the perp down the road. He got hit by a car but just got right back up and ran again. Drugs maybe. We need all eyes and ears out here. I'll keep looking but I don't know which direction he went."

"On it," Eoin said. "You might be right about the drugs too. Fratelli said he's pretty sure he shot the guy. Didn't slow him down for a second."

"Flak jacket?"

"Could be. Just be careful out there. This guy is dangerous. If he's amped up, even more so. I'm gonna call in the cavalry."

"Sounds good," Paulie told him. "We're gonna get this guy, Murphy. Even if it's not today, we're gonna get him."

"Yeah." Eoin hung up. Paulie turned to look at Taylor. "Let's just drive around and see if we can't see him." Even as he said it though, he felt it was futile. The killer was in the wind and he knew it. He got the impression that Taylor felt the same way because he didn't say anything. He just nodded and started driving.

8

Paulie and Taylor both frowned as they walked past the growing crowd. Ringold and Turner had their work cut out for them. Paulie stopped to talk to them. "Murphy should have told you I was coming," he said, showing his P.I. license. "He's with me."

"Go on." Ringold thumbed over his shoulder. A woman rushed forward and he stuck an arm out to block her. "Not you. Get back. Come on."

"Reporters are vultures," Taylor said as they approached the house. "And they're not even easy to pick out anymore because everyone and his brother has a blog or a TikTok these days."

"Yeah," was all Paulie said as they walked past an ambulance and some more officers on their way into the house.

"She's upstairs," one of the officers said to them.

"Thanks," Paulie said as they walked by.

They entered and found Eoin and his partner in the living room. "What the hell are you doing here?" Fratelli snapped angrily. "And who the fuck is this guy? There's been enough mess made of my crime scene."

Paulie smirked at him. "Your partner invited me, and this other guy is my partner."

"I knew you were coming, dipshit. I thought you were out there looking for our guy. I mean why are you *here*?"

"We did look. There's a ton of boys in blue out there. If he's going to be found, they'll find him. We didn't need to be driving around for hours. We need to see this body and figure out who this person is and why they're doing this and if we can, who's next."

"I'd say you're a regular Dick Tracey but I know you never would."

Paulie laughed. "That one actually would have been clever if I wasn't bi. I'd dick Tracey and trace my tongue over Dick's dick." Taylor clamped a hand over his mouth to keep from laughing.

"Alright, enough. I already got my brain beat in tonight. I don't need the bickering," Eoin said. "Here's what we got. Max said this woman wasn't the second victim. She actually came first."

"Max?" Taylor asked.

"The forensic pathologist," Paulie told him. "So we could have more then," he said then, addressing the group. "Who knows how many bodies are stuffed into closets around here?"

"Some of them might still be alive if we can find them," Taylor added.

"We don't know who this woman was," Fratelli told them. "There's nothing right now that proves she was one of yours, but she could have been. We need to look into it."

"One of mine?" Paulie asked, eyebrows raised.

"You know what I mean."

Eoin rolled his eyes and sighed. "She was an older woman, sixties if I had to guess. Strange time for someone to come out of the closet but I don't want to assume anything."

"You shouldn't," Taylor told him. "A lot of people from that generation lived in the closet even when they were straight. The rules were rigid and they couldn't be themselves. If she had a husband who recently passed, she might have seen her chance to fully be herself."

"That's a lot of speculation." Fratelli scratched his chin. "Is this guy licensed? Who the fuck is this guy?"

"I said already he's my partner. Let's focus on the case. We need to have all abandoned homes and buildings in the area searched for bodies. Hell, there may even be someone alive in one of them."

Before Fratelli could speak, Eoin jumped in. "He's right. We also need to look into the vics we have, see if there's anything that connects them, even if it's a cable guy, a hairdresser, whatever."

"That don't make sense," Fratelli said. "I thought all hairdressers were queer."

"Oh, can it," Paulie told him. "You guys have the resources so you check the buildings and houses. We'll look into the victims. We're gonna start with this one if you don't mind."

When they walked by, Fratelli hit Taylor with his shoulder. Taylor looked at him but kept going, following Paulie up the stairs.

"Fuck is your problem?" Eoin shook his head.

"I don't trust him," Fratelli answered. "He shouldn't be here, neither one of them."

Upstairs, Taylor said, "This place is creepy without anyone being murdered here."

161

"It was a home daycare," Paulie told him, "but yeah, abandoned, it's pretty creepy for sure. In here."

A photographer was taking photos and stopped, walking by them out of the room. Another officer said, "Place has been printed and combed. They'll be up in a minute to take her out," before following the photographer to the stairs.

"Got it," Paulie said, going into the room. He watched his step and made his way to the open closet. "Shit."

Taylor walked up behind him. He looked over Paulie's shoulder. "Poor old gal," he said.

She was frozen like a wax statue, hands in claws. The room was full of dried shit and piss, and dissolved organs. Her body was so misshapen it was hardly recognizable as human. Her eyes were wild, accusatory. "Her hands like that, she had to be scratching."

Paulie opened the door wider and looked at the inside of it. It was raked in rows and covered in dry blood. "I'd like to talk to Max and find out his take."

"I don't think Fratelli would allow that."

"Fuck him." Paulie looked at the inside wall of the closet. "Hey look. What's this?"

He moved out of the way so Taylor could get a better look. He shined a flashlight into the shadowed closet past the harshly staring dead woman and her claw-like hands. Something was scrawled, no...etched into the wall by her elbow. It looked like a cathead. Taylor frowned. "No way to know if she did it or if it had been done by a kid when this place was up and running."

"Maybe the boys downstairs can find some old photos of the place from when it was open."

"Do businesses normally take pictures of the inside of the closet? Say it was her. What could it mean?"

Paulie sighed. "Maybe she has a cat at home and she wanted people to know, to take care of it. That's definitely something my mother would have done."

Taylor nodded. "Or maybe she was trying to tell us something about who put her in there. A vet? Pet store employee? Cat sitter?" He took a picture of the drawing with his phone.

Paulie stared at the old woman's wrinkled flesh hanging from her bones with nothing to keep it on like a child wearing an adult's clothing. He looked at her dried-out tongue hanging limply from her mouth and a spider crawled over it. "Alright. Let's find out her name and address if we can. I wanna get out of here."

Taylor didn't argue. When they got down, they walked right past Fratelli and marched out into the fresh air. People passed them going the other way with a stretcher to collect the body. "Let's figure out if our first vic had any cat connection," Paulie said. He noticed that Taylor was looking a little green. "You good?"

"Yeah, I just... I don't miss this."

Paulie smiled at him and patted him on the shoulder. "A little bit you do."

Taylor snickered. "Mostly don't. I just want peace."

"You'll like it better working with me."

They walked past the gathering crowd and the caution tape to the car. "Oh yeah? Your ego coming back?"

"Nope. I just think you love what you do and you're good at it and when you're doing it with another queer person you'll find your peace."

"Maybe. No promises."

Paulie smiled at him but he looked back at the house and he could still see the old woman's fixed stare glaring like she was angry with him. *We're gonna find them. I promise.*

9

J OHN SAT AT HIS kitchen table staring at a beer he wasn't drinking. His wife was behind him rubbing his shoulders. "I know I hit the guy, Trudy. I'm old but I'm still a good shot. I know I hit him. There was no bullet, no blood, guy just runs off like he's fucking Superman or something."

"Maybe he is," Trudy says with a chuckle.

He turned to glare at her. "You think this is funny? We got a serial out there and it's a PR disaster cause they're killing queers."

Trudy released his shoulders with a pat and walked to the stove. "Sounds to me like they're taking out the trash. Let me cook you dinner."

John looked at her and frowned. It wasn't that he disagreed with her. He thought the ten thousand new genders and sexes were ridiculous and they were trying to turn all the kids into some kind of gay, but the nonchalance she had when remarking about people who were brutally murdered bothered him. She used to be the sensitive one out of the two of them. "That's a little harsh don't you think?"

He could smell the melting butter in the frying pan and he almost started salivating. She looked back over her shoulder at him while she continued. "I'm not saying they should be killed like that. I'm just saying we could do to lose a few, to go back to the way things used to be."

"Well don't go talking like that around people, alright? It's my job to catch this fuck. I don't need people thinking I'm turning a blind eye because of some shit you said to one of your girlfriends at the supermarket."

"Of course. You should try actually drinking that beer. Relax a little, you old grump."

***

Eoin stood over the body on the steel table and he frowned. "Why do people hurt the elderly?" he said. "They've already been through it. Their time is limited. Just let 'em have it."

A thin man with an even thinner mustache turned toward him. "I don't think the people who do shit like this are very empathetic, Murph."

"I know, but it just seems like even scumbags should have lines or a code or something. Tell me you have something useful, Max."

"Unfortunately, the autopsy just confirmed everything we already thought. She died of accelerated dehydration. Dead a while. Almost a week, I'd say." He lifted up a pair of dentures and made them open and clap shut like a Halloween gag. "Running the database on dental records?"

"You can get dental records from dentures?"

"They're designed to your mouth, to your bite. They match."

"Interesting. Let me know when you have something." Eoin didn't wait on a response. He left the room, walked down the hall, and out of the building. He took out his phone, but before he could use it, it rang and he almost dropped it in surprise. "Shit."

Eoin looked around hoping no one saw that and answered the phone. "Murphy."

"We found another one, Murph. Over on Hudson, the old factory. It's bad. You should get Fratelli and head over here."

"Shit. Alright. Give me a few. Don't let anyone remove anything until I get there."

Eoin hung up. Again he tried to call Fratelli and the phone rang. He shook his head in frustration and answered it. "You were right, Murphy. We found a body. It was in the old school house, symbolic maybe. This one's a kid, Murph. Sickening. Turner is in a bad way. I don't know how long he's gonna stick with this job."

"Can't really blame him," Eoin said into the phone. "We've already got another call to go to. I'm gonna send the P.I. over there. Give him the rundown and anything he needs."

"You got it."

When Eoin hung up he still didn't call John. Instead, he called Paulie. "We got two more. We're taking one. You and your boy take the other. We'll meet back at the station and share our findings."

"Fratelli good with that?" Paulie asked.

"He'll live. It's at the old schoolhouse. Vic is a kid, Paulie."

"Shit. I might leave Tay out of this one. Alright, I'll see you in a bit."

***

Standing in the doorway, Paulie watched Taylor get dressed. His eyes lingered a little too long on the man's boxer briefs and the treasures they contained, and he turned away, fixing his gaze on a picture on the nightstand. It wasn't a better choice as he believed it was a photo of the husband who had left. "It's alright if you wanna sit this one out," he said.

"I'm already in it, Paulie. Let's go."

Paulie looked at him dressed and could still see the body under the clothes. He cleared his throat and turned to exit. "I just don't want to break you on our first case."

Taylor snickered. "You're serious, aren't you? I'm not a P.I., Paulie."

"Yeah. About that." Paulie handed him a piece of paper.

"What's this?"

"You meet all the requirements for this state because of your time in law enforcement. You just have to sign and send and you're licensed."

"It can't be that easy."

"Can and is. I'm working on trademarking PC investigators but that's a bit more difficult."

Taylor sighed and signed the paper. "Let's go see about this kid."

"Alright, partner."

***

"You alright?" Eoin said from the driver's seat. "You seem grumpier than usual."

"What do you think? We're up to four dead with no suspects," John answered.

"Actually boys called with two more while I was waiting for your old ass. We have six total. The good news is—"

"There's good news?"

"They've checked every abandoned structure in town. Six is at least the end of it and we've got eyes on all of them. If he tries to add a seventh we'll know."

"That's shit but I'll take it. Now let's find the sonofabitch and nail him to the wall."

They pulled up at the factory and got out. A reporter was already on scene with a mic in their face. "Fuck outta here." John shoved him away.

They ducked under the tape and went in. "You know the weasel will probably press assault charges for that shove," Eoin said as they entered the building. There were people combing for evidence and taking photos all around.

"Let him. I ain't got shit to take. He gonna sue me for Trudy? He can have her."

"There it is. I knew something was up. You two fighting?"

"You can fuck off too. Someone show us where the dead guy is please."

"This way," an officer said, leading them through pipes and machines. John hugged himself against the cold.

"Drafty in this damn place."

They went down iron stairs to a basement level and past more machines. "Any idea what these things do?" Eoin asked, taking in their surroundings.

"No, sir. Closet's back here."

They had to duck under a thick pipe and John didn't quite duck fast enough. He cursed and grabbed his head. When the others turned they saw the anger in his gaze and turned back. When they reached the closet, Eoin looked away from the sight before him. "Christ. This has to be one of the first."

"There was more anger in the beginning." John stepped past his partner to look in the closet. "More violence."

"How can you tell? Guy's practically a skeleton," Eoin said.

"Bones are chipped and dented, broken in places, like the left side ribs. Look behind him. Back side of the skull is dented. Someone beat the shit out of this guy before locking him in here."

"Why would it change? Usually, it's the opposite. People grow more violent with their kills, not less."

"It started emotionally. The killer had a more emotional connection to this one. Then he decided to keep going. It became some kind of crusade, a job, something necessary."

"This closet was metal so there's no scrapings or carvings inside."

"Where's all his skin and organs, sir?" the cop who led them to the closet asked.

Eoin gestured to the stains on the floor and walls around the body. "Dissolved, rotted, gone. That's it now."

"Jeez."

"You need to get on the horn and ask Paulie if there was violence at their scene. We need to get over and see the other two," John said.

"On it," Eoin said, taking out his phone.

***

When Taylor and Paulie got to the school they couldn't believe it. The building was being attacked by kudzu. It looked like something out of a zombie apocalypse movie. "How the hell long has this place been abandoned?" Taylor asked.

"Since the seventies, I've been told. No one's bought the spot. It's just rotting like a body," Paulie told him.

"Speaking of," Taylor said. He led the way to the door and tugged it open. It came open with a creak. He looked over at Paulie as they stepped inside. "Something's nagging at me."

"Shoot."

"If the old woman came before David, why was the killer there when we got there? Why would they return to the scene of one of their older kills?"

"Maybe it wasn't the killer. Maybe they were a squatter with drugs on them or something."

Taylor shook his head. "If Fratelli says he shot the guy and there's no bullet or blood, then he was prepared, wearing a vest or something. That's not random squatter behavior."

"You think they planned to run into us?"

"I don't know. Maybe. What if they wanted to get in our heads or throw us off track, mess with us, or something."

Paulie was thinking about it when his phone rang. "Hey, Eoin."

"Look for signs of violence. We need to piece this together. Our first vic had been beaten before being locked away. It was aggressive. We're going to check on one of the others. If nothing else we might be able to create a timeline."

"Alright. Thanks for letting us know. You said there's another?"

"Two more actually."

"Shit. Okay. Anyone looking into vest sales? If your partner hit the guy, he had to be wearing something, something that kept the bullet. You can't just pick those up at Walmart."

"Already did. We got a list being compiled. We'll see if anyone on it connects to the vics somehow."

"Good. Keep us posted. We'll see you at the station."

He hung up and saw the look on Taylor's face. "Two more vics. They want us to look for violence and said their guy was brutalized before being locked away. The M.O. has changed. It could help us put together a timeline."

Taylor frowned. He looked at the ground. "The idea that we're walking to see a dead child that may have been brutally beaten and locked away until his death for being gay doesn't sit well with me. I feel sick."

"All the more reason to catch the bastard."

"Weird the press isn't crawling around."

An officer walked up to them. "You two the ones Eoin told me to look out for?"

"That's us." Pauli showed his ID. "It's quiet."

"Yeah, it seems everyone is at the other one where the detectives are. Don't worry. They'll find their way here before long. They always do."

"Did you find the kid?" Taylor asked him.

"Nah, my partner did. It messed him up pretty good. He's outside but I can get him if you need him. He's got a kid about the same age."

"No. Let him be," Paulie said. "Just tell him to keep an eye out for the swarm of vultures."

"Will do, boys. The body is in a closet on the third floor. Room 304. Forensics hasn't even gotten here yet so try not to touch anything or they'll have my ass."

"Got it. We have gloves and bags for our shoes. We both have a lot of experience with crime scenes."

"Good."

They watched him walk away and then they hunted for a stairwell. "Tay, over here," Paulie said. Taylor hurried to him as he opened the door. Then they looked up and down the stairwell to make sure no one was going to jump out at them, nodded to each other, and headed up. At the third floor, they stepped into the hall and both stopped to look around.

"This damn case has me on edge," Paulie said.

"I feel it too. It doesn't help that someone hit Murphy at that house."

"Yeah. Let's just find 304."

They both pulled gloves on and slipped bags over their shoes. Taylor found the room first and pushed open the door ushering Paulie inside. Paulie nodded and went past Taylor followed him in and eased the door shut gently as he would for a child who just went to sleep. The room itself was far different than the outside of the building. It looked like class could have just ended a minute ago. The map was down and there were children's drawings in chalk on the blackboard. One desk even had neatly arranged books on it. Paulie shivered. He pointed at the closet and they both approached without making a sound.

Paulie grabbed the knob and looked at Taylor. Then he turned it and opened the door. "Shit," he said, exhaling pent-up breath, his shoulders sagging.

"This has to be the most recent one," Taylor said. "Looks and smells like he just went."

"If we had been faster, found this kid yesterday or the day before, he might have lived." Paulie had tears in his voice.

The boy wasn't looking at them. He was staring up at something inside the closet with him, a look of terror on his sallowed face, sunken eyes surrounded by dark rings wide open. His lips were dried and cracked and hanging open for his swollen tongue to poke free like a turtle in a shell. The boy was nude, his body far too thin, ribs jutting out, bones showing through his skin. He was sitting in a sticky mess of his own excrement. It was on his fingers and lips like he had tried to re-ingest it to survive. "Looks like he vomited," Taylor said. "There are food pieces in the mess."

"What do you think he was staring at?" Paulie asked.

"Could have been anything. Dehydration causes hallucinations. Poor kid probably thought he was trapped in there with a monster or something."

"It was the monster that trapped him. Why didn't he scratch the door like the others?"

Taylor squatted and gently lifted the boy's hand to look at his shit-coated fingers. The fingernails were missing, every one of them. "He couldn't."

Paulie scrunched his face. "That means they saw the scratching as a problem to remedy but in most cases, it was just raking lines in the door. We need to dig deeper into the cat drawing."

"Maybe that's why they returned to an earlier scene. They knew we were headed there and there was something they didn't want us to find."

"We just have to hope it wasn't something else. If they did find and they got away we're screwed."

"That's very glass half empty of you. I thought you were the positive one," Taylor said.

"We're standing in front of a child who died of thirst. The glass is completely fucking empty, Tay."

"At least with him being fairly fresh, it shouldn't be hard to find out who he was."

"That's our silver lining?"

"It's what we have, Paulie."

***

John stood in front of the open closet in the basement of a house on the other side of town. He was shaking his head. "What is it?" Eoin asked him. "From where I'm standing it's just more of the same."

"I know this guy. Kyle his name was. No way he was queer. He worked with Trudy. Used to come by the house for drinks. I met his girlfriends, always gorgeous. He was rough around the edges not all proper like the gays are."

"Are you serious?"

"Yeah, what? Guy used to play rugby for god's sake."

"Gay people can't play rugby? What if everything you just mentioned was for show and that was the whole point because he was in the closet?"

John shook his head. "I'm telling you, Murph, this guy was straighter than my dick."

"Your dick doesn't have any curve to it?"

"The fuck you asking me that for? You trying to end up in one of these closets?"

"It's just us, Fratelli. You think the killer has the place bugged to make sure none of the investigators are queer?"

"I'll put you in the damn closet myself, you keep asking about my dick."

"Lovely. You said this guy worked with your wife. That means you're the first person we know for sure has a connection to the victims. How's that?"

"Oh, fuck you, Murphy."

John stormed away and Eoin smirked before moving in closer to the dead man. "What's this? Hey, asshole. Come over here."

Eoin checked to make sure his glove was tight, then he reached behind the naked man and pulled something from the floor. It was stuck in the dark black fecal matter. He pulled it free with a sucking sound and held it out for Fratelli to look at. "Some kind of necklace. Your straight guy must have shit it out after he was locked in. Why was it important enough for him to swallow?"

John stared at the dangling silver chain with internal bleeding made darkened feces sticking to it like gum. "Maybe that has to do with who gave it to him. We need to find out who that was."

"Don't rule out a boyfriend," Eoin said.

"Shit," John added with a sigh. "Charm is the symbol for Cancer. I hate that astrology bullshit but maybe it can help us figure out who it came from."

Eoin smiled at him. "Could be our first real lead."

John's phone rang. He answered it. "Fratelli."

"Hey, bud. It's Max. I'm here with the last victim. Female. Beaten beyond repair. I would have to do an autopsy but she may have died before she was even locked in the closet."

John blinked. "She old?"

"I'd say mid-twenties actually."

John huffed and scowled. "I mean time of death, Max. She a skeleton?"

"Oh," he said with a snicker. "She's not a full skeleton. She has some skin on her bones but it's definitely been a while, longer than the other two I've seen. Her organs were absorbed for water. They're dried up nothing."

"Alright. Thanks. Did you find anything else? Anything in the mess around the body?"

"Nope. All that is about gone. Mostly stains at this point. Odor is foul but that's about it. Did you two find something in the shit?"

"No, just wishful thinking."

"Oh, and I got a match on our second vic's dentures. Her name is Kathy Danvers."

John couldn't shake the feeling that that name was familiar for some reason and it bothered him. "Thanks, Max." He hung up and looked at Eoin. "Let's get back to the station and meet up with the queers so we can try to make sense of all this shit."

Eoin gave him a stern look but didn't say anything. He just shook his head, stood, and stormed past his partner out of the room.

John sighed and wiped sweat from his forehead. "Shit."

10

"I CAN'T STOP THINKING about that kid," Taylor said as they drove to the police station. "He couldn't have been more than ten or eleven. How could anyone do that?"

Paulie huffed. He looked out the window. "I don't know. Maybe they believed it was important, God's work or something."

Taylor shook his head. "I don't buy it. That's too easy. None of this works. We're missing something."

"I think we're missing a lot of somethings."

"I guess."

They pulled into the lot and parked, getting out quickly. On their way in, some officers waved and greeted them and others just stared angrily in their direction. "It seems our approval rating is pretty mixed on the most recent poll." Paulie grinned. Taylor just shook his head.

Eoin met them in the hall. "In here," he said, leading them into what looked like a boardroom with a big brown fake wood-grained table. There was a bulletin board nearby and John was sitting at the table with a file and a stack of papers spread out that he was poring through.

"Here's what we've got," Eoin said. "The whole area has been checked. We've uncovered six victims." He tacked a pic on the board. "Vic three was first, the most decomposed, and with signs of early violence and personal feelings." He tacked up another photo. "Vic six that Max called in about was next. Also brutally violent and slightly less decomposed." He tacked another photo. "Then the old woman, Kathy Danvers." He put up the next picture. "Then David." He put up a photo next to it. "Then Kyle." He put up one last photo and sighed. "...and then the kid."

"We checked missing persons," Paulie said. "Kid's parents have been a wreck. They were even on local news a while back. His name was Cole. Cole Matthews."

"Cole," Eoin said. He wrote it down on a piece of paper, tore it off, and added it to the board above his picture. "So we have a timeline and half of them have been identified already. We'll have the rest in a day or two."

"What do we have on them? Anything that connects them?"

"The opposite," Eoin said. "Fratelli swears Kyle was straight."

"Maybe he was." Taylor shrugged. "We had one vic we knew was gay in a closet. Perhaps we were too quick to jump on that connection."

John sighed and leaned back in his chair. He massaged his eyes. "So we have a gay guy, an old woman, a child, and some skeletons. Fuck."

"There's something," Paulie told him. "We saw a crude cat etching in the closet with Danvers. Originally, we let it go because it could have been done by the kids ages ago, but when we found Cole, his nails had been removed so he couldn't scratch. The killer saw the scratching as a problem and tried to fix it. Maybe that was why."

Eoin chimed in. "We found a necklace Kyle shat out. He must have swallowed it before they locked him in. It was the astrological symbol for Cancer. He thought it was important enough to eat it."

"Alright, this is good," Paulie said. "We need to find out who in Kyle's life was a cancer. And see if there was any cat connection with Danvers."

John slammed his palm on the table. In frustration, he smacked the papers across the tabletop. "So an old lady might have had a cat and Kyle, the man with a thousand girlfriends, knew someone born in the summer. We're minutes away from an arrest." He shoved his chair back and stood. "I need a goddamned cigarette." He stormed out of the room.

"He's not wrong," Taylor said. "It's not a lot. They could be out there working on vic seven now."

"We've got all abandoned properties being watched. I don't think he'll go out of jurisdiction because all six are here. Why stray now?"

"Unless there's already more other places," Paulie said.

"I already thought of that. I called the surrounding areas to see if they had anything that fit. Only one body stuffed in a closet and it was a hit, a turf thing, criminal against criminal, unrelated to ours."

"Well, that's a plus," Taylor said. "Alright. We'll head over to Danvers and see what we can find. Something has to give eventually."

"That's a good idea. Fratelli knew Kyle so we might have an easier time going that route, but...in the morning. It's been a long day. Let's all get some rest and attack it tomorrow with clear heads. Yeah."

"Alright," Paulie said. "It'll be easier to get a picture once the other vics are identified anyway. Then maybe we can figure out why they're in the order they're in."

"I'll put a rush on Max," Eoin said. "I don't think that guy sleeps anyway."

★★★

John pushed his way into his apartment and kicked his shoes off. Trudy was sitting on the couch with her feet in fuzzy slippers up on the coffee table. She had the TV on playing reruns of Sex and the City, and a cup of cocoa with marshmallows in her hand. "Hot cocoa?" he questioned.

She shrugged. "I wanted something hot and it's way too late for coffee. I'd never sleep."

"They make decaf."

"Is something wrong? You've had a long day. Your dinner is in the oven where it's been for a long time."

John crossed to the kitchen. He opened the oven door and looked at the pan, then closed it again. Instead, he opened the fridge and grabbed a bottle of beer, closed the door, and selected the opener magnet stuck to it. He popped the top off the bottle. It hit the counter and ricocheted into the sink. John left it there and walked back to the living room.

"Kyle is dead. I found his body today."

"Kyle?"

"Stop it." He took a sip of beer and wished it was something stronger.

"Like Kyle from my old job?"

"Yes. Kyle that's been over here a hundred times. Kyle whose house we've been to a hundred times. Kyle."

"Wow. That sucks, huh? He was a good kid."

"That's it?"

Trudy looked at him with confusion. She leaned forward, grabbed the remote, and shut off the TV. "Are you looking for me to say something? It sucks. I hate that he's dead. It must have been hard for you to find the body of someone you knew. I'm sorry you had a hard day. Did I get it?"

"No, Trudy, you didn't." He took another sip of beer and walked around to stand before her. "I want you to tell me why Kyle shit out your fucking necklace as he lay dying in a goddamned closet!"

Trudy paled. "What?"

"Your cancer necklace, the one your sister gave you for your birthday when we were still Kyle's age. Why the fuck did it come out my vic's ass, Trudy?"

"It-it could have been someone else's. People could easily have the same necklace."

John's facial muscles twitched. He stomped towards the bedroom. Trudy jumped up from the couch. One of her slippers fell off and she stepped awkwardly. "Where are you going?"

"To look at your jewelry."

She ran after him into the bedroom. "Alright, okay, listen. John, listen, okay? I lost it. It's the truth. Before I left my job, when I was retiring, something you need to do, they had a going away party for me, cake and everything, lots of booze. The necklace came off that night. I have no idea where. I guess somehow Kyle ended up with it."

John sighed. He sat down on the edge of the bed and shook his head. "And it was important enough for him to swallow it when he was being murdered? You need to come clean with me, Trudy, because so help me God if you had anything to do with this—"

"Then what, John? You're gonna leave me? You're gonna hit me like your piece of shit brother did his wife until she left him? What? What are you gonna do, John?"

"My goddamn job, Trudy. I will take you out of her in handcuffs myself."

"Because of a necklace? That's it? Forty years be damned?"

John snarled. He jumped up from the bed fast enough to make her dart backward away from him with a gasp. "Just tell me the fucking truth. I have six bodies, Trudy, and the only connection to any of them so far is my own goddamn wife."

Huffing, Trudy stormed to the kitchen and grabbed herself a beer, abandoning her cocoa. She brought it back and stood before him with one hand on her hip. "Fine. You want the truth? The truth is that you're old, fat, and tired all the damn time and we haven't had sex in years. Kyle was young and virile and ready to go. So we fucked. A lot. That's how I lost my necklace. Happy you got the truth?"

John released a steady stream of air like a deflating balloon. "So what? Was he in love with you? He kept the necklace and swallowed it so the killer couldn't take it when they stripped him. Why would he do that?"

"He said he was but I didn't believe him. Hell, I could have been his mother. He had so many women. What would he want with me? I had a life and a husband. I just wanted to get laid and feel alive again. I guess maybe his feelings were real. I don't know."

John walked past her and put his shoes back on. "You guess maybe his feelings were real, and you want to talk to me about forty years. It was gross hearing the way you were talking the other day and then I find your necklace at a crime scene. Now you tell me you were screwing my vic. What's next?"

Trudy laughed in his face. It was aggressive and without humor. "So because I said we could do with a few less queers, I'm a murderer now? You know I was talking to your old partner, Chris, and—"

"What the fuck are you talking to him for? You fucking him too?"

"He was a friend for years, John. I'm not going to throw people away because they got a different job."

"He was a dirty cop, Trudy. He got fired. He did terrible shit behind my back, but then again I guess it would make sense that you were friends."

She scoffed at him. "The point is, he said you were working with queers on this one, that you're all buddy-buddy with a couple of—"

"Stop! That piece of shit shouldn't know who I'm working with or what I'm doing, and what the fuck does it matter to me who a detective fucks? I care if they solve cases, goddamn it."

"I wouldn't be surprised if your new partner was gay. He isn't married. For years he hasn't brought girlfriends around. He lives by himself and he admits to being a Swifty."

John's mouth fell open. He felt like his brain was broken. "Eoin? I can't even listen to you anymore. Just shut up. I'm going out. And for the record, Taylor Swift is very good at what she does, and her early country stuff is very honest and charming."

"Wow...that sounds like something your fag partner would say."

John lunged forward. He raised his hand by her face but stopped himself when he spied her smile. "Do it," she said. "Do it and I'll make sure you're the one that leaves here in cuffs, not me."

John said nothing else. He just walked out and slammed the door.

***

Eoin rubbed the sleep from his eyes. He didn't bother putting a shirt on. Someone was banging at his door. Pants would have to do. He opened it and saw John. He looked haggard and his eyes were wet. "Come in," he said. "Beer?"

"Actually, do you have anything stronger?" John said, closing the door behind him.

"I have just the thing," Eoin said with a smile. He went into the dining room, opened the bottom of the china cabinet, and pulled out a bottle. He stood and wagged it. "Maker's Mark."

"Perfect. Bring glasses though. I don't want your cooties."

Eoin laughed and shook his head but did as John asked. Then he joined him on the couch. "Case getting' to ya, huh?"

John gave a humorless laugh. He poured a glass of bourbon and held it up. "In a roundabout way, I guess. That necklace you found... It was Trudy's."

Eoin stared with wide eyes as John knocked back the glass of bourbon. "You didn't say anything?" He poured his own glass.

"I wanted to talk to her first."

"And?"

"And she was banging Kyle. He was in love with her."

"Shit."

"Yeah. She hates the LGB whatever stuff more than most people too, Murph. I hope she's not involved in this somehow, but I feel like I don't even know her anymore."

"I don't think Trudy could murder, Fratelli. Do you?"

"She's been hanging around with Chris. He was as dirty as dirty gets. Who knows what she's capable of?"

Eoin blinked and emptied his glass, then refilled both. "Seems like Kyle was definitely straight though. Guess you were right on that one."

"Seems so, though Trudy said she thinks you're queer."

"Me?"

"Yup. You live alone and aren't married and listen to Taylor Swift. Case closed. I actually defended Taylor by the way."

Eoin laughed. It was genuine and loud in the silent room. John joined in and they clinked glasses and drank more. "You know," Eoin told him, "I am part of the community, just not how she thinks."

"What's that mean?" John sipped at the contents of his glass.

"Alright, listen. Almost nobody knows but... My dead name is Heather."

John stared at him for a moment. He said nothing. He drank his bourbon, refilled it, and drank more. "Fratelli?"

"John."

"Alright. John. You good?"

John rubbed at his mouth. "So you said you're not gay, but you used to be a girl so you were gay then and now you're straight?"

Eoin took a deep breath. "In a simplified way I guess, sure, but I've always been a straight guy, just in the wrong body. I fixed that."

John knocked back another shot and rubbed his face. "So do you have a..."

Eoin rolled his eyes and sighed. "Why is that everyone's first question to a trans person? Why does it matter what's in my pants?"

"It matters," John said, refilling Eoin's glass and handing it to him, "because you said you're straight so if you date a girl and she's straight then she will be wanting a penis, right? And if you don't have one then..."

Eoin waved his hands. "Stop. Just stop. Everyone I've ever dated, I've been upfront with so they knew before anything happened. But I am post-op now, since last year."

John's eyes went wide. "No shit? When you took that leave of absence?"

Eoin nodded. John laughed and shook his head. "You asshole. You told me your aunt Sally died. I was upset. I met her."

"It wouldn't have been very believable if I made someone up no one'd ever met."

"Tell that to poor Sally everyone thinks is dead. This is a fucked-up day of my partners dropping truth bombs on me. Why didn't you just tell me the truth?"

Eoin sighed. He drank from his glass. "You're pretty open about how you don't love queer people, John."

John shrugged. "I mean, yeah, in general, but that don't apply to you."

"Why not? Why dislike Paulie and Taylor but be just fine with me?"

"Paulie is a cheater and a liar and I don't like that, especially tonight. Taylor, I don't know and I'm not inclined to trust strangers for obvious reasons. You... You're my partner, Murph, my brother. My life just imploded and where did I go?"

"Would you have still come if you knew?"

"Of course."

Eoin felt shocked. He looked at the big man sitting across from him holding his glass up for a toast and he couldn't believe this moment was happening. "Well color me surprised, John. I'm sorry I didn't tell you sooner."

They clinked glasses and drank. "I get it," John said. "Why you didn't tell me? I know it has to be scary, telling someone like me something like that. I'm glad you trusted me with it and especially tonight. I needed that. Just more proof we're brothers."

Eoin wiped tears from his eyes. "Did you really defend Taylor Swift?"

"I did," John said with a laugh. "I don't know why. I was just so mad and it just came out."

Eoin cracked up laughing too. He refreshed their glasses. "To Taylor Swift," he said.

Laughing, John said, "To Taylor Swift," and clicked his glass with Eoin's.

11

As Paulie opened the gate to the chain link fence surrounding the one-story lime green house, Taylor said, "You get any sleep last night?"

"Not a wink. If we don't find anything here, we've got nothing, nothing but bodies."

"So we've got to find something here."

They closed the gate and headed up the stone path to the three steps leading to the front door. Paulie knocked.

"Didn't she live by herself? That's what Eoin said before we left this morning," Taylor said.

"Yup, but there's a car out front. I just don't want to barge in on someone."

"Could be a neighbor. It's out front and not in the driveway."

"Could be but I don't want to find out by opening the door and getting a gun in the face." He knocked again. "Anyone in there? Police."

The door opened and a thirty-something brunette woman was standing before them looking them over. "So you finally came to tell me," she said.

"I'm sorry?" Paulie said, flashing his ID.

"My mother. I watch the news. You'd think you would tell me first, but you would also think you would catch the killers."

"We're really sorry," Taylor told her. "That's what we're trying to do now. Can we please come in? There might be something inside that can help us."

When she stepped aside to let them in, Paulie said, "I really am sorry you found out by the news. We just got her name last night. I don't know how it even got to them. I didn't know until you told me. I avoid TV."

The woman frowned. "It's alright. I'm Janice. I came here when I heard about my mother. I needed to be sure. Then I couldn't bring myself to leave. I just keep looking at things, remembering things."

"So you had a good relationship?" Taylor asked. When he got an angry glare, he said, "I'm only asking because the only way I would know anything about either of my parents would be if it was on the news."

"We weren't like 'call every day' close but yeah, we got along. Every time we were together it was good. Now, I'm wishing we had talked more."

"I'm sorry," Paulie said. "Do you know anyone that would want to hurt her?"

"No, not at all. My mother was as vanilla, and wholesome as they come. Besides, according to the news, it's a serial killer. They said my mother was one of six."

Taylor sighed and rubbed at his face. "Damn them."

Paulie said, "Janice, even serial killers have connections to their victims a lot of the time. They chose those people for a reason. That reason, that connection, that's what we need to figure out."

The woman started crying and turned away from them. "It's a lot. It's too much. It's insane. My mother was good. She was good."

"I know. It's not fair. It's not right. It's not."

Janice wiped at her eyes and sniffled. "Well, it wasn't my dad. He died a year ago. Now I have no parents. I have no parents." Her voice got quiet and she found her way to a chair, falling into it.

Taylor noticed an open book on the table beside her chair. It wasn't a novel. It looked more like a journal. "What's that?" he asked. "That you're reading."

Janice sniffled. She wiped her nose and cleared her throat. "It was my mother's. I found it last night. There was so much I didn't know."

"Do you mind?" Paulie asked, gesturing towards the book.

She shook her head. "Go ahead."

When he took the book, Taylor said, "Janice, if it's alright with you, I'd like to look around a bit."

She tossed her arms up lazily and let them fall back to the chair. Taylor nodded. "I'll try not to disturb anything and I'll put it all back exactly as it was. I promise."

"Thank you," she mumbled, wiping her eyes again.

Paulie read some of the book. He flipped forward and read some more. "I know this is very personal, a connection to your mother, but do you mind if we take it with us? It could really help with the case and I'll make sure it gets back to you when this is all over."

CHISTO HEALY

Janice bit her lip and fresh tears came but she nodded. "Yeah, okay," she said quietly.

Taylor went room by room and searched for anything that could help. "Did your mother have a cat by chance?" he called to Janice as he searched. He certainly didn't see any bowls or beds.

"A cat? No. She didn't have any pets. No."

Paulie put the journal in his pocket and joined the search. An hour later they were offering their condolences to Janice, thanking her for her cooperation and heading back to the car.

"Nothing," Taylor said when they got it. "Everything in that house was typical suburban old lady. We don't have anything more than we did when we got here."

"Not true," Paulie said as he started the car. He reached into his pocket and threw Kathy Danvers' journal onto Taylor's lap. "Read a few weeks before the end. It was a Wednesday, I think."

Taylor flipped through the book as Paulie drove. "Holy shit," he said. "Old lady Danvers really was gay, but according to her own words, she never told a soul and wrote it to finally speak her truth. Maybe we need to look a little deeper into daughter Janice."

"For sure, but first we're going to visit Cole's parents. We have something linking two of the victims. We need to see if it's the same for the third."

***

"Terry Stillwell, and Tammy Collins," Max said. Terry was the first. He was a real estate agent for Downtown Quality Homes. Tammy was second. She was a personal trainer at Manny's Fitness. Both were reported missing a long time ago. Now they're found." He took a bit out of an egg salad sandwich.

"Thanks, Max," John said. He looked at the bodies on the tables. "If Terry was first and he was a real estate guy, he would have access to the abandoned properties in town. Maybe our killer who was clearly angry at him for whatever reason got the information from him or stole it and used it to start their crusade."

"We need to find out more about Mr. Stillwell, see who had the fury and passion to beat him and lock him in a closet."

"Let us know if you find anything else," John said as he hurried out of the room.

"Thanks, Max," Eoin said with a wave as he ran behind him.

"You're welcome," Max said back in garbled words with his mouth full of egg salad.

12

COLE'S MOTHER WAS LEANING into the arm of the couch and sobbing like the furniture was the supportive husband she longed for.

"I'm so sorry," Paulie said to her. "I can't imagine what you're going through. We really want to catch the person who did this, but we need your help. Can you tell us what you remember about the day he went missing?"

She sniffed and sat up some but continued to clutch the couch arm like it was a grounding hand. "He got into an argument with his father. Cole told us he was non-binary and wanted to be called they/them. Lance got so mad. He said those were plural pronouns not for one person. He asked if Cole was gay now too and Cole said he didn't want to have sex with anybody and ran out of the house. We never saw our boy again."

Paulie and Taylor exchanged a glance. Taylor spoke. "Mrs. Matthews, I know this is hard but I have to ask. Do you think there's any way Lance could have hurt Cole?"

She shook her head, cried some more, leaned into the couch, wiped her eyes, and said, "Lance would never hurt him. He loved him. He was scared for him. You know? Those types of kids are never happy. They get beat up and don't give us grandkids. It's just hard."

"There are ways for LGBT people to have kids, Sandra," Paulie said with a frown. "You didn't report him missing for a while. Why?"

She sat up with an angry glare on her tears-streaked pink face. "We thought he just went to his uncle. Joe is a fa— He's one of those people. He's Lance's brother and one of the reasons Lance was so scared for his son."

"He lives local?"

"Right down the goddamn road. That's probably how Cole got those ideas and learned all that queer stuff. I hate that sonofabitch."

Taylor sighed but he said, "Can we assume his name is also Matthews?"

"No you cannot," she spit venomously. "That fairy married his boyfriend. His last name is Carlson."

"Thank you for your time, Mrs. Matthews. Again, sorry for your loss," Paulie said. As they headed for the door, Taylor mumbled, "Fairies are magical beings. They're pretty awesome." Paulie took his hand and they walked outside.

***

John scowled when the door chimed loudly. He looked at the woman sitting at the front desk and showed her his badge. "Did you know Terry Stillwell?"

She blinked in surprise and said, "Everyone knew Terry. Nothing has been the same since he left. That guy made this place what it was."

Eoin stepped around John and smiled. "Hi. I'm Detective Murphy. You said he left? Where did he go?"

The woman blinked again. She looked away. When she looked back, she gave a big smile. "Well, I don't know per se, but I assumed to start his own agency somewhere. He was meant to be someone big, that guy."

"He's dead," John said plainly. "Not too big. Any idea who would want to hurt him?"

The woman's mouth fell open. She stumbled for a moment like she'd forgotten how to speak. Then she cleared her throat. "I-I don't know. A lot of people were jealous of him but I can't imagine... Are you saying Terry was murdered?"

John nodded.

She shook her head. "No. I don't know. I'm sorry."

Eoin asked, "Did he have any romantic relationships that you know of?"

The woman found her smile again. "No, no. Plenty of women tried, myself included, but Terry was never interested. He was just focused on his career, I suppose." She gave an awkward laugh.

"And what was your name, ma'am?"

"Tammy. Tammy White."

John nodded. "Thanks, Tammy. Call us if you think of anything useful." He dropped a card on her desk and turned to Eoin. "I think we ought to go check his house."

***

Paulie smiled when the front door opened. "Are you Joe Carlson, sir?"

The man looked Paulie and Taylor up and down, cringed with distaste, and said, "I am. Who the hell are you?"

Paulie smiled again. "I'm Detective Paisano and this is Detective Conroy. We're investigating what happened to your nephew, Cole."

The man's demeanor instantly changed. He hurriedly stepped aside. "Please come in. How can I help?"

He led them to a glass table and offered them tea but they both declined. When they were all seated, Taylor said, "Your sister-in-law said they didn't report Cole missing right away because they thought he was with you."

Joe sighed. "So he *was* gay? That's the only reason they would expect him to come to me."

"Non-binary ace it sounds like from what his mother said," Paulie answered. "But the impression I got is it's all the same to her and your brother."

"My brother's a piece of shit," Joe said. "I'm surprised he didn't beat him like he did me when I came out."

The detectives shared a look. "So Lance was violent?"

"Lance is a homophobic prick to the nth degree. Asshole put me in the hospital when he caught me with my first boyfriend. Cole is a good

200

kid though. I've been sick since they went missing. I haven't slept. If my brother hurt them, I'll kill him myself."

Taylor frowned. "We found Cole, Joe. I'm so sorry."

"What?" The man started trembling. "Cole's... Cole's... Did he do it? Did Lance do it?"

Paulie put a hand to his mouth. Taylor continued, "We don't know. I know you're angry and hurt, but you can't take the law into your own hands, Joe. You have to let us handle it."

Joe's face twitched. "Oh yeah? Like when my best friend Lynn got beaten and left half-dead in a grocery store parking lot and the fucking cop who showed up left without so much as writing a report because she was trans? Fuck you. The law doesn't give a shit about us."

Paulie wiped tears from his eyes. "We're not with the police, Joe. We were but we left... Both of us. We started our own agency. We're private detectives. I promise you...we will not let Cole down. Please trust us."

"I think you should go. I have to go to work in a few minutes."

Paulie nodded. "Okay. I'm so sorry about Cole."

Joe said nothing. He just led them both to the door.

***

Eoin was in the kitchen opening cabinets with gloved hands. "Everything is here," John said from the adjacent room. "He certainly didn't seem like a guy leaving for a career upgrade."

"Yeah. I'm guessing that's just the theory they came up with to make themselves feel better."

"You see anything actually useful?"

"Not yet."

"His computer is here but I'm no good at that shit. You wanna take a look or should we just bring it back and let Miranda have a crack at it."

"Both," Eoin said as he entered the room. He took a seat in front of the laptop. "You keep looking around."

John made his way to Terry's bedroom. "Definitely looks like the desk lady's story checks out. This guy was more into real estate than relationships. He's got housing books by the bed. No pictures of anyone."

"They're on here," Eoin called back. "He's got pictures of him and a blonde woman. They definitely look more than friends. Seems she lives in Massachusetts. He wasn't uninterested in women. He was in a long-distance relationship."

"So he wasn't gay?"

"Doesn't seem like it. He's got documents of love poems he wrote for her. Loretta."

"And he was the first? Makes me think we've got this all wrong?"

"Yeah."

John felt the back wall of the closet and it gave him pause. He felt around some more until he found what he was looking for and tugged. The back of the closet came away. There was a duffel bag. John reached for it and was surprised by the weight of it. He unzipped it and looked inside. "Holy shit. Murph! Come get a look at this."

Eoin left the computer open with a photo of Terry and Loretta as the wallpaper and he ran to see what John had found. The bag was full of stacks of hundred-dollar bills. "Either the guy didn't believe in banks or he was into something shady," John said.

"Maybe he planned to move to Massachusetts and start over with Loretta."

"The kind of anger... The beating he took, it speaks of passion, of rage...jealousy, a broken heart."

"Or maybe of someone who'd been robbed or screwed over."

"Alright. I'm gonna call this in and get forensics over here."

13

PAULIE AND TAYLOR WALKED into the police station. They got more smiles and waves than dirty looks this time which they each silently took note of. They went straight to the boardroom where Murphy and Fratelli were waiting. "We've got something," Paulie said when they entered.

Eoin gestured towards the empty seats across the table. "We've got something too."

"But you first," John told them.

"Danvers had just come out of the closet but hadn't told a soul, only wrote it in her diary," Taylor said. "Her daughter was there reading it, said she heard about her mom on the TV and came to go through her things. I'd say that makes her a suspect."

"Cole had just come out too, the day they went missing," Paulie added. "They told their parents they were non-binary. Their father, Lance, is a big-time homophobe with a history of violence too. This thing is coming together."

"Until it isn't," John said.

"What do you mean?"

"Our first vic, Terry Stillwell. Not gay. Also had a giant bag full of money hidden behind a wall in his closet, and the woman at the desk of his old job said a lot of people were jealous of him."

Both P.I.s gave a deflated sigh. "I don't get it," Taylor said. "If he was the first, he should have set the tone, the M.O., everything. Why would he be the only one that wasn't part of the queer community?"

"What about vic two?"

"Tammy, the personal trainer. We still need to look into her, but finding the monkey wrench that was Terry made us come back and try to start over."

"Shit," Paulie said. He turned his head sideways and rubbed at his forehead.

The door opened and a woman that was all of four feet tall walked into the room. She had brown pigtails popping out from under a baseball cap and big thick-rimmed glasses. "What do you have for me boys?"

"Hey, Miranda," Eoin said. "We've got Terry's computer. We already found some interesting stuff on it but we need to know if there's stuff in the places we can't see. What kind of skeletons did this guy have in his closet?" He gestured toward the laptop on the table.

"On it. By the way, Max said your girl Tammy had the bisexual flag tatted on her calf. Thought you might want to know."

John slapped the table in frustration. "Easy, Fratelli," Eoin said. "Thanks, Miranda."

"Oh, hey, Miranda," Paulie said before she could leave. "Can you do us a favor and get us whatever info you can find on Kathy Danvers' daughter Janice?"

Miranda gave a great big smile. "Oh, sure, that one's easy. Kathy Danvers doesn't have a daughter named Janice." Everyone was staring at her. She turned and looked over her shoulder. "What?"

"Are you sure?" Taylor asked.

"Positive. I've already looked into her. She didn't have a daughter Janice because she didn't have a daughter at all. She had a son named Dan. Dan Danvers." She chuckled. "Who could forget a name like that?"

"Is it possible Janice is trans?" Eoin asked. "Could Dan by her dead name?"

"Nope. Dan is still Dan. Has his own auto repair shop on Calloway."

"So who the fuck did we talk to? She was in Danvers' house?" Paulie said.

Miranda shrugged. "Dunno."

"Well, looks like we need to go see Mr. Danvers," Taylor said. "You two wanna come?"

John shook his head. "Nah. Me and Murph are gonna go back to the real estate company and talk to Tammy at the desk again, see if we can't shake something useful out of her now that we know more about Terry."

"I'll call you when I'm done digging through Mr. Stillwell's digital closet," Miranda said cheerfully.

14

PAULIE AND TAYLOR WALKED up to the car shop. There were several guys out front in coveralls working on a pick-up truck and a sedan. Another guy, equally greasy, was at the counter dealing with customers. "Hey, fellas," Paulie said. "We're looking for Dan Danvers. Is he around?"

"What for?" a dark-haired man with a scar in his right eyebrow said.

"We're detectives investigating his mother's case," Taylor said.

The man nodded. Then he threw a wrench at them and took off running. "Fuck. Why did he run?" Paulie shouted. Then he and Taylor gave chase.

***

John pushed his way into the real estate office with Eoin a step behind him. Tammy wasn't at the desk. A thin man with even thinner glasses was sitting there in her stead. "Maybe it's her day off?" Eoin whispered.

"Hey, where's Tammy? We need to speak with her?" John said, flashing his badge.

"Who's Tammy?" the man said.

"The woman who was sitting right where you are, yesterday," John said angrily.

"Oh, Rebecca? She quit."

"She said her name was Tammy," John snapped. "Now, why would she do that?"

The man shrank in on himself. "I don't know. How would I know?"

"What does Rebecca look like?" Eoin asked. After the man gave a nervously hurried description, he said, "That's her, Fratelli."

"Did she give a reason for quitting?" John asked.

The man shook his head. "She just walked out. I don't know."

"Shit," Eoin said.

John put his palms on the desk and leaned in close to the man's face. "We're gonna need to know where she lives and what she drives. Now."

***

"Why are you running? Stop running!" Paulie called as he sprinted after Dan.

"Keep after him. I'm gonna go around and cut him off," Taylor said as he swerved and took off down a side street.

Paulie was running hard but Danvers was running harder, like his life depended on it. "We just want to talk to you. Just stop!"

He ran into traffic on the main road and was weaving between cars. "Shit," Paulie said, hitting the brakes as a truck sped by inches from him, their horn blaring. He cringed waiting for his moment to cross. When it finally came, he cursed and ran. When he got to the other side of the street, he could see Taylor at the far corner. Danvers was on the ground. Panting and holding a stitch in his side, Paulie ran over to them. "Careful," Taylor said as he drew near.

Paulie saw then that Taylor was bleeding and holding his side. Dan was clutching a knife. "Stay the fuck away from me."

"What the hell are you doing, man?" Paulie asked, shaking his head. "We just wanted to talk to you and you're running through traffic and stabbing people?"

He pointed the knife at Paulie. "Just stay back."

"We're investigating what happened to your mother. She's dead, Dan. When we went to her house, there was a woman there. She said her name was Janice. Tell us who Janice is, Dan."

Dan started crying. He didn't say anything. Just sobbed. Then he lifted the knife and dragged it across his own throat. Blood spewed out all over his shirt and the ground.

"What the fuck?" Paulie cried. He ran over to the man but Danvers swung the knife at him, making him back up. He swung it at the air until he collapsed on his face, blood running across the pavement and his eyes still sad and staring lifelessly.

"Fuck!" Paulie shouted.

"He's with his mother now," Taylor said. "And I need a doctor."

***

John banged on the apartment door. "Open up, Rebecca. Police."

He looked at Eoin and back at the door as he knocked again. There was a crash inside. "Dammit. Stay here," Eoin said, running down the stairs and around the building.

John shrugged. "Good. I didn't want to be the one to run. I'm too old for that shit."

He listened a moment longer, then shouted, "Rebecca, I'm coming in!"

John kicked the door and it didn't budge. He grimaced, rolled his neck, and tried again. On the second kick, the door came flying open. It wasn't hard to see that the woman was trying to leave in a hurry. Her open suitcase was on the table next to a half-empty bottle of liquor. Her clothes and things were all over the apartment strewn about like the place had been robbed. He wondered if that was intentional. "Rebecca, you in here?"

He heard Eoin shouting, "Down on the ground! Now!" and John hurried to the bedroom in the back. There was a broken lamp on the floor and the window was open. She must have kicked the lamp on her way out. John went to the window and leaned out. The woman who had told them her name was Tammy was standing about fifty yards from Eoin who had his gun drawn and pointed in her direction. "Do not try to run, I will shoot you," Eoin said. "Get down on the ground. Keep your hands where I can see them."

John huffed. He walked out of the apartment, lit a cigarette, and hobbled down the stairs, smoking as he went. When he got around the building, Eoin looked at him and threw his arms in the air. Rebecca was on the ground in handcuffs. "What? I'm old. I could hear you from the window. You had it. You did fine," John said.

He walked up to the woman on the ground and squatted to look her in the face. "Now you wanna tell us why you gave us a fake name, a name that happened to be the same as one of our victims?"

"I was confused."

"You were confused as to what your own name was."

Eoin grabbed her and hoisted her to her feet. He read Rebecca her rights and dragged her to the car. "Are you charging me with lying?" she asked. "Or moving? Is that a crime now?"

When the detectives got in the car, Eoin said, "Help us understand, Rebecca. What are you running from? What really happened to Terry?"

She sat in the back seat, cuffed and staring daggers. "I don't what happened to that queer fuck. I hope they all die."

"Holy shit," John said, "You thought he was gay. Why? Cause he wouldn't date you? Are you such a catch that any man who doesn't want you has to be gay?" He laughed.

"What? What are you talking about?" she demanded.

Eoin looked back at her. "Terry wasn't gay, Rebecca. He just didn't want you."

"Well, I want my lawyer."

John sighed. "That's fine. When we tie you to all six murders they'll bury you underneath the jail."

"What? I don't even know those other people and I didn't kill Terry."

Eoin's phone rang. He answered it. "Hey, Miranda."

"I found some shit on your boy's computer, and you're gonna wanna gather the troops and see this in person."

"What kind of shit?"

"Some serious dark web kinda shit, man. Just get back here."

When Eoin hung up, he turned to face the woman in the back seat. "You know what that was? Evidence. Good call on the lawyer, Rebecca because you're going away for a long time."

She didn't say anything but he watched her in the rearview mirror and she looked nervous. *Good,* he thought. Then the phone rang again.

★★★

"What the hell happened?" John stormed over.

"They took Taylor by ambulance," Paulie said. "Guy stabbed him before he offed himself. He didn't even want to be a detective or get involved in any of this shit. I pushed him and now he got stabbed."

"How bad is it?" Eoin asked.

"I don't know. I mean he was lucid but shortly after the guy died, Tay collapsed. I just hope he's alright."

"Why did this guy slit his own damn throat?" John wanted to know.

Paulie shook his head. "I don't know. We just asked for him and he ran. Tay tackled him, got stabbed, and then dude opened himself up. It was the craziest thing. Even as he was bleeding out, he swung his knife at me. It was like he wanted to make sure he died."

"Sounds like he's as guilty as that one." John gestured with his thumb at Rebecca who was watching from the backseat of their car.

"Maybe he was," Paulie said. "He's not much of anything anymore."

"That woman's name isn't Tammy. She lied and tried to skip town. We caught her on her way out," Eoin said. Paulie looked at the covered body and the blood stains on the concrete. "How are they connected?"

"We're damn sure going to find out," John answered. "Miranda says she's got something big. She wouldn't say it over the phone. She said for us all to come in."

Paulie wiped some tension from his face. "Alright. I'll go check on Tay and meet you over there. Hopefully, it'll be both of us."

Eoin patted his shoulder. "Good luck, brother. See you soon."

Paulie glanced back at the body and all that blood, and then he went to his car.

Max waved at him. "You're good. Hope your partner is okay. Everything you said checks out from what I can see. The wound was definitely self-inflicted."

"Thanks, Max," Paulie said. Then he got in the car and drove away.

15

PAULIE WALKED INTO THE hospital room. Taylor was sitting up and smiling which Paulie took as a good sign. "How you feeling?" he asked as he sat in the chair by the bed.

"Like a guy who was just stabbed," Taylor said, his smile widening. "Nah. I'm alright. They said it nicked my liver so I gotta be careful, and gave me some preemptive antibiotics to protect against infection. I'll be good as new in no time."

"Good," Paulie said, finding his own smile. "There's been some leads." He filled Taylor in on Rebecca, then said, "Miranda said she's got something big. She wants us there to see it in person. I'll represent our agency and then come by later or tomorrow to fill you in."

"Like hell. Either turn around or see me naked because I'm getting dressed and going with you."

"Is that really my choice or did you really just mean turn around?"

Taylor sighed. "You haven't earned my nudity yet. I need at least a pina colada but I'd prefer some Thai curry tofu, the yellow kind, and a foot rub, and not like the two-minute kind like the real deal 'break out the oils' kind. So yes, the choice is yours."

Paulie turned around. "Sheesh. Whose got the ego now?" He could hear Taylor's discomfort as he moaned and groaned, struggling to get into his clothes. "So, tell me the truth. Did you really just not want me to see how bad the wound was so I wouldn't make you stay?"

Taylor gasped and Paulie whipped around worried only to find him dressed and smiling. "You really are a detective," Taylor said.

"And you're an asshole."

"Sometimes. Let's go." Paulie followed him out into the hall where a nurse stopped them.

"Mr. Conroy, you are going against doctor's orders if you leave this hospital."

"Noted." He walked around her.

"You have to sign the paperwork acknowledging that."

"Have it sent to the police station. I'll make sure he signs it and returns it."

"It's not a permission slip for a field trip, sir," the nurse said angrily.

"That's exactly what it is," Paulie countered. Then he hurried to get in the elevator with Taylor before the doors closed.

***

When they walked into the board room, Fratelli and Murphy both reacted with care and surprise. "How are you feeling?"

"Where'd he get you?"

"They got you on painkillers? You better not drive."

"Those things can be addictive too so be careful."

"I'm fine. I've been hurt worse. What's Miranda's news?"

"We don't know," John said. "She insisted we wait to see if you two were gonna show before she filled us in."

"Oh man," Paulie said. "I bet you loved that."

"Let's not start," Eoin told him and Paulie put up his hands defensively.

"You get anything out of Rebecca?" Taylor asked.

"She lawyered up, and we're probably gonna have to let her go, but we'll get her. That chick is dirtier than a homeless man's ass crack."

"Wow...thank you for the imagery, John. I appreciate it."

"After the church does taco Tuesday at the soup kitchen," he added.

"What do we know about her?" Paulie asked. "Not nearly as much as we know about homeless men's assholes, apparently."

"We know she had romantic feelings towards Terry, vic number one, and she got rejected," Eoin told him. "She thought he was gay and let her true feelings about that be known. Turns out, she's not a fan."

"So you think this all started from a broken heart? She blamed the whole community and kept going after she killed him?" Taylor asked.

"I'd love to make her for all six," John said, "but when Murphy teased her with that, she seemed genuinely surprised. Hers was more violent than the rest. I think she did hers out of passion and jealousy and then someone else took the idea and ran with it."

Eoin added, "There's also the giant bag of money and the long-distance girlfriend in Terry's life. I don't feel like the money was a coincidence."

"Dan knew who Janice was," Taylor told them. "When we had him and asked who the woman was in his mother's house, that's when he freaked out and slit his own throat. He was definitely in on something bad and it involves that Janice woman who pretended to be his sister, and quite convincingly too I might add."

"She was crying and everything," Paulie said.

"There was a serial killer who used to call the police and cry every time he killed. Tears don't mean shit," John said.

"The weepy-voiced killer," Miranda said as she entered the room carrying Terry's laptop. "Paul was something else. Did you guys know—"

"Miranda, let's focus on this investigation," Eoin said. "What do you have for us?"

She smiled. "It's actually way worse than what we were already talking about. Also, I probably shouldn't be smiling when I say that. I'm sorry. So, before I actually show you what I found because it's really disturbing shit, I want to go on record and say I know that Terry was a victim but he was a bad dude and into some really fucked up stuff."

"Like what?" Paulie asked.

"Well, I'll show you." She opened the laptop, typed some, and then turned it around on the table so they could all see it.

"What are we looking at?" John asked her.

"The Dark Web, boys. This was a pain in my ass to get into. Everything is encrypted and pinged off of random IP addresses as well as rigged with viruses like digital guard dogs. Serious shit, I'm telling you."

"Okay, so this serious shit... What is it? Looks like some kind of forum?" Eoin chimed in.

"It's a group, the C.C.C. or the Coalition for Creating Comfort."

"That is definitely not an evil-sounding name," Paulie said with a nervous laugh.

"I think that's the point, blend in, stay off the radar. They could have meetings at hotels and no one would bat an eye, but the real truth of who they are is in the hidden stuff."

"Who are they?" Taylor asked.

"People who want to create comfort for themselves by removing the thing that makes them uncomfortable, i.e. queer folk."

"So they're Nazis or something?" Eoin asked.

Miranda shook her head. "No. They're everyone. They're dentists, doctors, lawyers, factory workers, cashiers, cooks, housewives, stay-at-home dads, the every man."

"Wait, and Terry was part of this group?"

"Oh yeah, big time. The idea is to nip it in the bud and remove someone as soon as they come out before they can," she made air quotes with her fingers, "become a problem. You can do it yourself or if you don't have the stomach for it, there's forums like this on where you can list the person and let someone else take care of it."

"I think I'm gonna be sick," Taylor said. "Maybe I should have stayed at the hospital."

"They're actually waging war against us," Paulie muttered. "And what? Murdering queer people gains you clout?"

"Oh yeah. Each person has a rating like online sellers and Uber drivers and the like. When you do well and kill a lot you have a high rating. If you chicken out, your rating drops."

"Christ," John said, looking at Eoin.

Eoin shook his head. "And there's a lot of these people? They're everywhere?"

"Countrywide it seems. Plenty in our own area as you've gathered. And I haven't even gotten to the worst part yet."

"This was the warm up?" Taylor said. He pulled out a chair and sat down.

"'Fraid so."

"Well, you might as well hit us with it," Paulie said, taking a seat of his own.

Miranda nodded. She turned the laptop towards her, typed some more, and then spun it back so they could see it again. "This is the gallery where you can share your kills and get tips and criticisms. They have likes and the sick fucks comment on the lighting and music choices."

She reached over and scrolled down. "All of these are murderers of LGBT people?" Eoin asked, his voice hushed.

"Every single one and it scrolls for a long time... A really long time."

Taylor had tears running down his face. "What's the point? Why are we doing what we do?"

"Because these people need to be caught and put away," John said firmly.

Paulie shook his head. "No, he's right. We're fighting a losing battle. We're outnumbered."

"Excuse me," Eoin said to him, "but fuck that. We fight a war the moment we realize we're different, the moment we are born into this world. Going to school is a war, going to work is a war, trying to date is a war, walking down the fucking street as the gender we actually are is a fucking war, and we do it because it's important, because we deserve to live, to love, to fucking be... So we've been fighting our entire lives, we're used to it, and we're not going to stop now." He turned to Miranda. "Did Terry kill someone?"

"He sure did and it's pretty damn gruesome. I don't think you want to see it."

"We need to," Paulie told her. "We need to understand what is going on around here."

"Alright, but I warned you." She spun the laptop to face her and scrolled up. Then she stopped on the video she was looking for, made it full screen, and spun it back. When they were all watching she reached around and tapped PLAY.

The video was of a young girl, maybe fourteen or fifteen years old. She was sitting on a park bench. Terry walked over and sat beside her. "How are you, Maggie?" he asked.

"Scared," the girl said.

"Have you told your parents yet? That you like girls?"

The child shook her head. "I know they'll be mad. They'll tell me it goes against God. Honestly, I haven't told anyone. I'm so glad you caught me because it means someone knows and I'm not so alone in this."

"I'm glad too," Terry said. Paulie's hands curled into fists on the table.

"You've known my parents forever. Do you think you could tell them? Maybe you can help them understand."

"I've got something I want to show you that I think will help with this whole thing," Terry told the child. Taylor turned away but turned back with his hand over his mouth.

They watched as Terry led the girl deeper into the park. They went into an area with lots of closely grown trees. "What is it you want to show me, Mr. Stillwell?"

"I'm going to spare you parents so many years of pain and embarrassment, save you from all the shame and pain you will feel trying to live as you are."

"What are you saying? Mr. Stillwell?"

She turned around to face him and whatever camera he wore. "I think someone else is filming this shit, watching and doing nothing," Eoin said. "Sometimes the camera is at his back."

When the child turned to face him, Terry swung a thick tree branch and hit her in the face. She fell to the ground and he brought that stick down on her face again and again. She was broken, bleeding, and raising her hands defensively. Her swollen eyes were crying. "Why?" she moaned through split lips, blood running over them from her broken teeth and ripped gums. "Why are you hurting me?"

"Oh, I'm not, sweetie. I'm killing you," Terry said. Then he went about mercilessly beating her with that ball-bat-sized tree chunk. He stomped on her viciously and kicked at her. Still, she crawled and grasped at the rocks and grass, trying to get away.

"For fuck's sake, enough. Turn it off," Eoin said. "I can't."

Miranda took a deep breath as she stopped the video. "You'd be surprised to see how much longer it goes. He doesn't quit and that kid wouldn't quit either. She just kept fighting to stay alive. It's the worst damn thing I've ever seen."

Taylor lunged for the garbage can and vomited.

"Fucking monster deserved what he got," John said.

"What happened to her?" Paulie asked. "To the body?"

Miranda frowned. "He kicked it into the stream. She floats down into the sewer pipe. She's probably still down there."

"Fuck." Taylor wiped his puke-covered lips with his sleeve. He got up and stormed out of the room.

"Tay!" Paulie called after him.

"Let him go," Eoin said. "He'll come back. He just needs time."

"Alright, so Terry was part of this group. He kills this kid. Then he packs a bag full of money and plans to skip town and go live happily ever after with his long-distance girlfriend," John said. "So where does Rebecca fit in?"

"A bag of money he stole from the real estate company he worked for. It's all on this bad boy," she said, patting the laptop. "I'd bet you anything, Rebecca was in on it."

"Sonofabitch," Eoin said. "She knew he wasn't gay. She knew he was going to skip town and ditch her after she helped him steal all that money. Maybe she even found out he had a girlfriend where he was going. He used her and she was pissed. Hell hath no fury like a woman scorned."

"Now all we have to do is prove it," Paulie said.

"We've got a warrant," Eoin told him. "We need to get over to Rebecca's place tonight and search it before we have to let her go tomorrow. Maybe she'll have a computer of her own with damning evidence on it."

John leaned over towards Miranda. "Are there videos of our other vics on here? That would be all the evidence we need."

"There's no video of Terry's murder but there is a post in the forum requesting it and guess what? It's posted by his own tag. The group probably didn't realize he was asking to kill himself because he used his real name and no one does. They have tags and character emojis... Avatars."

"You think the guilt got to him?" Paulie asked.

"No. I think someone else used his login and his group membership to have him killed."

"Christ. That would explain him not being gay," John said. "It was Rebecca. I know it. I'm taking that warrant over to her place now. I'll show the apartment manager so someone official knows it's legal."

"I'm gonna check on Tay," Paulie said.

"I'll keep digging and see what I can find. Maybe the other vics are on here," Miranda said. "There's a lot to sift through."

"I couldn't do it," Eoin told her.

"I'm fucked in the head already," she told him with a shrug of her shoulders. "When it's over, I'll find a nice boy and fuck til I forget."

"Whatever works for you, I guess."

"Naked boys, vodka, and horror movies."

Paulie made a thoughtful look, then said, "Same."

"Oh yeah?"

"Well, girls or boys, and whiskey instead of vodka these days, but pretty much, yeah."

They shared a laugh. "Well, when the job is done, maybe we should celebrate together," Miranda said with a wink in Paulie's direction.

"We need to get more warrants, subpoena the computers and phones of David's parents and wife, and Cole's parents. We need to see if they're tied to this C.C.C. before it's out in the open. Once it's out, they'll get rid of everything and cover their backs. Someone needs to talk to people who knew our personal trainer too. I'd be willing to bet that someone in her life is tied to that damn group too. I'll talk to the captain on the way out, see if he's got someone to spare."

"I can do it." Miranda smiled. "I gotta pass his office anyway. We're gonna nail these people. It's just a matter of time."

When Miranda and John left the room. Paulie looked at Eoin. "Your speech earlier..."

"Oh yeah, that probably felt patronizing to you when you didn't know I was part of the community. I am."

"No, I knew you were as soon as I heard the pain in your voice when you said those words. I wanted to say you were right. Just like the child in Terry's video, even when it's completely hopeless, we can't stop fighting."

Eoin reached out and smacked Paulie's arm. "We can't save the world in a day. Let's start by saving our town."

"Hell yeah. You going with John over to Rebecca's?"

"No. I've got my own warrant. I'm going over to Dan Danvers' place to see if I can figure out what he was running from and who Janice is."

"Wait...you said Janice?"

"Yeah, that's what you two said she told you her name was."

"I've got to find Miranda. I'll call you."

Paulie ran from the room. Eoin sighed. Behind his eyes he saw that beaten child struggling to get away, fighting for her life as a grown man beat her senselessly, and not just any man but the one she trusted with her secret. He looked over at the bulletin board with the photo of Terry's beaten skeleton and he sighed. Then he walked out of the room as well.

16

P AULIE LOOKED AT THE door. He wanted to go check on Taylor.
It was his fault the man was even involved in all this and saw that
video, but he couldn't go to him yet. Puking probably hurt his stab
wound, maybe even opened it. *Soon,* Paulie told himself. *I won't be
long.*

He went around the building looking for Miranda. No one seemed
too inclined to help him. He didn't know whether they didn't like him
because he was queer or if they didn't like him because he was a P.I..
Either was believable.

One person even told him Miranda had gone home for the day.
Eventually, he found her office on his own, in the basement of the
building. He was already frustrated and upset so the sounds of the
horrific videos she was watching when he walked up didn't help his
mood any. He knocked on the open door and she turned away from
the screen in time to miss a man getting bludgeoned with a hammer.
Paulie saw it over her shoulder and it twisted his stomach.

"Hey, sorry to bother you," he said.

"I said when the job is done," she told him.

Paulie startled. "What? Oh no. I'm not here for you er uh for that. I have a question about something I saw when you were showing us the forum earlier."

"Oh. Well, that is equal parts disappointing and relieving. How can I help you, Detective Paisano?"

"When we were at Kathy Danvers', her daughter who wasn't her daughter said her name was Janice. Now I could have sworn I saw Janice a bunch in that forum."

Miranda sighed. "You did, but it's not going to narrow things down. Remember I said there were emojis you could use? There are a few avatars to choose from. Ed, Steve, Karen, and Janice. For obvious reasons, more people choose Janice than Karen."

"So Janice is a codename for these people who kill queer folk?"

"Yup. Janice for the females and mostly Ed for the males."

"Shit. So the woman at Kathy Danvers' house was definitely connected to the C.C.C. but she could have literally been anyone."

"I'm afraid so. It could have even been the person who killed her."

"In that case, get me a sketch artist," Paulie said, silently apologizing to Taylor.

***

John left the warrant with the apartment manager and he went upstairs to properly search Rebecca's house this time. He found the laptop under the couch and put it on the table. Then he went through the rest of the house. He didn't know what he expected to find. She was smart. She used his computer and his own account and group to put the hit out on him. She even acted like she thought he was gay and tried to sell her hatred. John didn't believe that she actually did hate the gays. She was just hiding behind bigotry.

Someone who covered their ass that well didn't strike him as the type to keep souvenirs or evidence on hand. A thorough search just reinforced his theory, so he took the laptop and left. Hopefully, it had what they needed to put Rebecca away. Poor Miranda had her work cut out for her.

His phone rang as he was unlocking the car. "Fratelli."

"Hey, John. It's Captain Marlowe. Miranda filled me in so I went to look into Tammy and see what I could dig up."

"We already know about the tatt. Max told us. Well technically he told Miranda and she told us."

"Well, her boss at the gym thought that tatt meant she should be willing to be with him despite having a girlfriend like being bi automatically means also being poly."

"Captain, I don't even know what those words mean."

"It means he thought because she was bisexual that she should be willing to cheat on her girlfriend with him and when she wasn't, he got mad."

"So he killed her?"

"Dunno yet, but he looks good for it. I'm working on confiscating his work and home computers to see if we can't tie him to that C.C.C."

"I didn't find anything at Rebecca's place but I'm bringing her computer back too. Looks like Miranda is gonna be the hero of this story."

"Everyone had done well, even the outside help. Now let's close this thing."

"Happily," John said.

***

Taylor walked the park looking every which way. His heart was racing. He found a section of closely grown trees and felt it had to be the right place. His heart sank when he didn't see any blood stains on the grass, any evidence of the terrible things that happened there. It felt wrong, unfair, that someone—a child no less—could be treated so unfairly and have it washed away by some rainy days, eaten by the neighborhood animals.

He squatted close to the ground and felt for any piece of her, a fingernail, a strand of hair, anything, but there was only grass and dirt like the girl had never existed.

Taylor stood. He walked to the stream and saw how it went right down a pipe into the sewer. It wasn't a pretty stream, a romantic place. It was just a giant filter. There was a true stream, a creek on the other side of the park. There were even fish in it, little ones. But this one, this one was for garbage. That's what someone's child had been reduced to just for being who she was. His soul was screaming.

Taylor stepped into the filthy stream and sat in the brown water. He slid down the pipe. When he hit the bottom he landed in water and slid down onto his bottom. In his mind, he saw that child, beaten and broken crashing into this filth and he screamed. It reverberated off of the tunnel walls.

Taylor got to his feet, his clothes dripping, and he started forward. He didn't care if he had to search for hours or days even, he wasn't going back up without the girl.

***

Eoin showed up at the house. Dan was dead but he didn't know if the man had a partner or kids. He realized he should have brought officers with him for backup, but this case had become personal to him. More people meant more opportunities for mistakes. When no one answered, tucked the warrant back into his pocket and broke the door in. He tried the light switch but nothing happened. Dan's death was too fresh for the power to have been turned off.

Eoin drew his firearm. "Anybody home? This is the police. If you're in here, please come out."

Silence.

Chewing on his lip, Eoin took out his flashlight. He looked all around for anything he could find that would tell him anything about Kathy Danvers. In the side pouch of the recliner, next to the television remote was a phone. It looked like a burner ol' Dan forgot to burn. Eoin laughed when he realized he didn't even need to crack it. There was no passcode, no fingerprint, no facial recognition, nothing. Dan wasn't a very good criminal. Maybe he knew it and realized he was going to get caught and that's why he did what he did.

There was only one conversation on the phone between the owner and a Janice.

"Shit." Eoin started scrolling and reading messages.

JANICE

It's done. As you requested, I didn't upload the video. It is just for you.

"Jesus. That's why he didn't get rid of the phone. The sick fuck probably kept watching it, watching his mother die."

Eoin felt compelled to play the video. Poor Kathy Danvers was apologizing when she did nothing wrong. She was begging Janice to take care of her cat, to please not let him starve. She choked as she was force fed the laxatives. "Why? Why is this happening?" was the last thing the old woman said before she was forced inside the closet.

Janice leaned by the door. "Because your shameful desires disgraced your family. Your son sends his regards."

Janice left the shot but the camera remained on the closet so Dan could listen to his mother sob for a while knowing that her own child did this to her. Did he find that satisfying? Is that why he kept it and continued to watch it? Danvers did have a cat. Was that why Janice was at the house when Paulie and Taylor showed up? She removed the cat and all evidence of it. Maybe they came to get rid of the carving but the police beat them to it so they had to do the harder thing and get rid of the actual animal, its litter boxes and toys, food and all evidence it existed.

Eoin couldn't help but wonder what happened to the animal. Did they kill it? Why? Because it was loved by a gay woman? Was that enough? Even for pets? It got deep under his skin. They already imprisoned the woman and left her to die a horrible grisly death. Disrespecting her final wish and disposing of her beloved cat seemed beyond cruel to him. He didn't just want to catch these people. He hated them.

Something crashed in the bedroom. Eoin drew his gun. "Police. Come out now," he called as he crept towards the back of the house. Something in his gut told him to get out but his anger after watching the video propelled him forward.

He entered the dark bedroom. The window was open and the curtain was blowing. He swept the room with his flashlight. "I heard you. Come out now!"

There was a thump to his right.

Eoin whirled around. On the floor by the nightstand was a black and white cat. Eoin was crying before he even realized it. He took the cat. The asshole took the cat. But now he went and ended himself. Who was going to take care of it?

"Hey." He made small kissy sounds as he slowly got down near the ground, encouraging the cat to him. "How would you like to come back to the station with me? Hmm?"

The cat looked up at him and mewed. Eoin smiled. He wiped his eyes and reached out to scratch the animal between the ears. It purred softly.

"You're a good baby, aren't you?" he said. Then something hit him hard in the back of the head and the world went dark.

17

TAYLOR STUMBLED THROUGH THE damp, cold tunnels stopping occasionally to run his hands through the filth at his feet. He didn't want to miss her. Could she have been eaten by something? He shook his head. She was here and he would see her buried properly. He only hoped her parents would do right by her this time.

He got more and more anxious the longer he traipsed through the muck. Taylor roared and punched the wall. He cursed and fell to his knees not caring about how dirty and wet he got. He lowered his head and cried. His hands fell into the water. His fingers felt something. It felt like hair. He moved his hands and felt it wrap around him, weaving through his fingers. Taylor let out a silent gasp and felt further.

"Oh god, oh god," he said as his fingertips felt her head. She felt so small for a girl her age. Taylor stood lifting the corpse out of the water. She was already so gone, so rotted that the flesh fell from her small bones into the sludge at his feet. Still, he stroked her exposed skull.

"I'm so sorry," he said to her soothingly. "I'm so sorry. You are loved and respected and I hope where you are now, you can see that."

Taylor knew he couldn't make it back up the pipe with her and he wasn't letting her go. He called Paulie, his voice still choked up from crying. "Are you at the station? I've got her."

"Got her? Who?"

"That poor girl. I can't get her up. I need you to send help to retrieve her."

"I got you. Hang tight."

***

Paulie thanked Ringold, clapping his arm. He turned back to Miranda. "Taylor found the girl from the video. She can at least have the respect of a proper burial now."

"I hate when it's kids," Miranda said. "I've watched hours of these videos now and I think that one will be stuck in my head for life."

"Yeah."

The artist, an older woman named Kelly, handed a paper to Miranda. She smiled at Paulie as she stood and left the room. "This is your Janice?" Miranda said, looking at the paper.

Paulie walked over and looked down at the paper she was holding. "Wow. Yeah. That's her. That's like perfect."

"Kelly is good. Paisano, I've seen this woman."

"You have? In life or in the videos?"

"The videos. A bunch of them. From all different areas. Apparently, she travels for this shit. She has to be someone big then, right? Like one of the founders or leaders or some shit?"

Paulie shook his head. "Or just their most viral superstar. Either way, if we take her down, we can put a dent in this thing. I know we can't stop it. We can't end it. Not realistically. But taking her down will let the rest know they're not invincible. War isn't won in a single battle, but it's a start."

"Well you know she's in town. Hell, maybe this is even her home base. If it is and she's this prevalent of a killer, she's probably got a criminal record. She had to be caught for something along the way even if it's just a DUI. I'll put the sketch in the computer and run facial recognition."

"Let me know if you get a hit. I'm gonna go make sure Taylor's okay... Finally. At least I know where he is."

"You got it. I feel excited now. Let's take this bitch down."

★★★

John cursed and shoved his phone in his pocket. He saw Paisano getting in his car and wondered if he should stop him but decided against it. He just huffed and stomped into the building. "Any of you seen Murphy?" he asked.

There were heads shaking all around the room and people murmuring. "Is there a fucking secret I should know about?" John snapped.

"No one's seen him," Turner said, swallowing hard.

"Well, get ready. We're heading over to Danvers' house and you're coming with me," John said as he passed the young officer's desk and crossed the room.

"Me, sir?"

"I didn't stutter. We're leaving in five."

"Shouldn't make fun of people with a stutter," Turner mumbled. John glared at him, then headed downstairs to find Miranda.

She had things going on several computers when he walked in. The largest screen had a video of a screaming person being forced into a closet paused at their moment of horror. "This is Rebecca's computer," he said, placing it on a nearby table. "I need you to find something on it to nail her with before they try to release her in the morning."

"I'm never this busy." Miranda smiled. "It feels so good to be included."

"Glad I can help. You haven't heard anything from Murphy, have you? I've been calling him since I left Rebecca's and I can't get him. It's not like him."

Miranda frowned. "Not a word. Sorry. But I can get right on this while I'm waiting for a ping on the facial recognition."

"Who's that?"

"Janice. She was the one at Kathy Danvers' place when the P.I.s were there. She's also the star of a lot of these snuff videos."

"Shit. Alright. I'm heading over to Dan Danvers' house and taking Turner with me for backup. Keep me posted."

"You got it."

John marched back upstairs. "Turner, with me," he said. Somebody was laughing and the room went quiet. John looked over at a guy named Richards who looked guilty. He stomped over his way. "Seems like you told a joke, I missed. I want to laugh too. Please, tell it again."

"I didn't say nothing, Fratelli. Just go find your girlfriend."

"Excuse me?" John was trembling so badly he could barely contain it.

"Franklin said your partner used to be a girl, that he bought his balls unlike the rest of us who were born with 'em."

"Oh yeah?" John said. "Hm." He punched Richards in the nose, then grabbed the back of his head and slammed his face into his desk. Then he addressed the room. "Eoin Murphy is a stand-up guy who I trust with my fucking life. He could be in danger right now because he puts the job first. I don't care where he got his balls, they're bigger than all of yours and if any of you fucking guys have anything to say about him I will personally kick your fucking teeth in. Is that clear?"

Most stayed silent. One cop said, "Fuck you, Fratelli."

John went to his desk and stood before him. "You think cause I'm old and fat, you can take me? Stand up and say it again."

"Just get the fuck out of here."

John slapped him so hard he fell out of his chair.

The officer looked up at him. "What the fuck, man?"

"I thought you were fucking tough? Weren't you a tough guy? Franklin ain't here, so when you see him, tell him his ass is grass. He should transfer. That goes for anybody else who wants to disrespect my partner."

The room was so quiet you could hear a pin drop. Even the two injured officers ceased moaning to look up at him in silence.

"Turner, let's go." John watched the young man scramble to his feet and hurry to leave with him. The room remained silent as the door fell closed.

18

Paulie stood beside Taylor who was seated on the curb in front of the park, still dripping sewage. "I'd hug you, but you stink. Seriously, you okay?"

Taylor looked up at him. In a hushed, choked voice, he managed, "Not even close."

Paulie nodded. "The Janice woman we met at Danvers' is a big player in this C.C.C. and if we can take her down it'll be a big blow to their little group. You did a good thing here today. Let's do another."

Taylor looked at him with thoughtful eyes. Then he nodded. "You should have seen her parents, Paulie. They were so relieved just to have her, even in that horrid condition. They sobbed and held each other and talked about what a great kid she was. I'm sitting here listening and I wanted to say, 'She was killed because she was gay,' and watch their demeanor change, but I couldn't do that to her. I wanted her to have her parents' love one more time."

"You did the right thing," Paulie said. "There's no point in it now. Nothing good would come from it. It wouldn't even make you feel better. You would have been disgusted and more upset than you already are."

"You're right."

"Okay then, let's get you a shower and a change of clothes, and maybe by then Miranda will have gotten a ping on the facial recognition and we can go catch us a bad guy."

Taylor sighed and stood up. "Alright. Let's go."

"You're driving though, pal, cause you're not sitting in my car."

"That's fair."

***

"You're gonna get in trouble for hitting those guys," Turner said in the car as John drove.

"What do you know about it?"

"Just that there's conduct regulations."

"You're new, kid, and I appreciate your innocence even if it's naive. Stay golden, ponyboy."

He pulled up in front of the house, right behind Eoin's car. "Isn't that Murphy's car?" Turner said.

"Yeah. So stay sharp, be ready. If he's still here and he's not answering, something is wrong."

"Yes, sir."

His phone rang and he jumped. Turner was on his way out of the car but John held up a finger to tell him to wait. He answered his phone. "What have you got, Miranda?"

"Exactly what you wanted. There was nothing on Rebecca's hard drive worth a damn but I checked her email. I didn't even have to hack into it. She had all her passwords saved. There's some juicy correspondence between her and Terry."

"I'm in a hurry, Miranda. Can you speed this up and get to the good part?"

"Right, sorry. Rebecca stole the money for Terry on the promise of partnership in the agency he was going to start with it. When she found out he was trying to skip town to start a new life with his girlfriend, she was righteously pissed. She straight up said she was gonna kill him, Fratelli. Her words were I'll kill you just like you did that queer girl. She knew. Kept her promise too. He didn't respond to any of her emails and I'll bet he never even opened them."

"That's practically a confession. Great work, Miranda. Show the captain. Make sure she gets charged. She's not going home anytime soon."

He hung up and found Turner looking at him. John sighed. "The woman in our lockup, Rebecca, she used our first vic's murder group to have him killed because they were embezzling money together and he planned to ditch her. At least one of six is solved. Well, two probably because the guy whose house we're at right now slit his throat when the cops tried to question him and one of the key players in vic one's murder group was in his mother's house when the private detectives went there. Now you're all caught up. Let's go find my partner."

Turner looked shocked and lost but he nodded and said, "Yes, sir."

They got out of the car. John went to Eoin's car and shined his flashlight in. It seemed no different than usual, no blood, no signs of a struggle. He sighed. When he headed for the house, he whispered to Turner, "Stay with me. Watch your back."

When they got to the door it was ajar. John turned and looked at Turner, the warning evident in his eyes. Then he turned back and pushed the door inward.

***

Paulie was sitting on the edge of Taylor's bed. He was staring at his phone waiting for his partner to get out of the shower. More importantly, he was waiting for Miranda to tell him the next step, where to go, and how to take this woman down. It felt like a fist was squeezing his heart. He could still hear the shower running and he sighed. Part of him had to admit that he would have loved to strip down and climb in there with him, but now certainly wasn't the time for that. His phone went off and startled him from his lustful thoughts. Paulie fumbled with it and dropped it on the floor. He bent over and snatched it up, answering it hurriedly.

"Hey, Paisano, this is Captain Marlowe from the precinct."

Paulie was stunned for a moment. He was expecting Miranda, not the captain. "What can I do for you, Captain?"

He listened as the captain to a long breath. "Listen, I really appreciate all the help you guys have given us on this case. It's been huge."

Paulie closed his eyes and sighed. "But?"

"We've got a bit of a mess on our hands right now and it's messier because it was you two who were involved, not official police, so I think it's time for you to step away."

"Captain, with all due respect, we didn't do anything to provoke Dan Danvers. It could have happened to anyone, and technically, it is official police business because Eoin contacted us, hired us on your behalf, and signed a contract. It's as much our case as yours."

"Look, Paisano, we hired you, we'll pay you, but we don't need you anymore. Dan Danvers was just the start. We just got a call that Cole's uncle shot and killed his dad. In a roundabout way, he said you inspired him with your visit."

"Shit. And it's *they*. Cole was non-binary."

"Yeah, okay. So take the money and run."

"I can't. We can't. Not yet. We have a chance to help bring down a person responsible for God knows how many queer people's deaths. It's almost over. Just let us finish it."

"I can't. I've got two people dead, both of whom were not victims of the killer and both of whom died after a meeting with you. You're gonna have to trust us to finish this one. When it's all over and we've done damage control with the mess you two have gotten yourselves in, we'll all go out for a beer. Until then, you're done."

Paulie knew arguing wasn't going to do any good. The captain's mind was made up. He hung up the phone. "Fuck," he grumbled. Then he said it louder. "Fuck." And he threw his phone against the wall.

***

John realized the power was out. Had it been cut? He didn't like any of this. It didn't sit right with him. He knew in his gut that something terrible had happened but he wasn't ready to face it. He used hand gestures with Turner to search the house using flashlights. They moved slowly and cautiously through every room, checking in and under everything. When the house had been swept, they returned to the living room.

"Shit," John growled.

"He's not here," Turner said. "No one is."

"I noticed that," John snapped. "But where the fuck is he?"

John took out his phone and called Eoin again. It went straight to voicemail. "Fuck!"

"Are you okay, sir?"

"No, Turner, I'm not. My partner came here and now he's gone and his car is still parked outside."

The young officer frowned. "I saw blood in the bedroom and broken glass. It smells like cat piss in there."

John looked at him. Then he hurried to the bedroom. There was blood but it was minimal, could have been from anything. There was no blood on the broken glass. It did smell like cat piss. The cat could have been responsible for whatever was broken. It could have even been responsible for the blood. It wasn't enough.

"Hey, Fratelli, I found something."

John hurried back and Turner handed him a phone. "It was under the chair."

John looked at it. "Holy shit. Eoin probably found this before we did. He wanted me to find it so when he was taken he tossed it. Good job, kid. This is evidence, proof. This is why Dan Danvers killed himself. He had his own mother killed, the rotten bastard."

"Doesn't do much good. He can't be charged. He's dead. And this doesn't bring us any closer to finding Murphy."

"It does do good because it will let the other people who cared for Kathy Danvers know what happened and it will get the two P.I.s off the hook in the court of public opinion. I'm gonna try to track Murphy's phone. Maybe it will lead us to him."

Turner said nothing. He just waited for John to use the app which took much longer than it should have because John wasn't very tech savvy.

"Shit. It says it's here," John said.

Turner helped him search until they found the phone in a bush out front. "Now what?"

"I don't know, kid." John went back to the car and used his radio. "I need all eyes on abandoned buildings and houses. Someone is bringing one of our own to one of them. The second you see them you take them down."

"We have all those places under surveillance. You still think they'll try it?"

"I think they've probably already fucking done it." *Hang in there, Eoin. I will find you.*

19

TAYLOR CAME OUT OF the bathroom wrapped in a towel and saw Paulie sitting on the edge of the bed with his face buried in his hands, his phone on the floor a few feet away with a cracked screen. Taylor put a damp hand on Paulie's shoulder. "What happened?"

"We're out. It's over," Paulie said without lifting his head.

Taylor's lips moved wordlessly for a moment, then: "Why?"

Paulie finally looked up. His eyes were red and puffy. He sniffed. "Fuckin' Uncle Joe went and shot Cody's dad and gave the impression we sparked the idea."

Taylor sighed and sat next to him. "Damn him," he huffed. "We told him to let us handle it. Asshole probably was guilty too. He was probably part of that damned C.C.C."

"Yeah," Paulie said. "So was Dan and now two killers are dead instead of behind bars because of our involvement."

"That what they said or what you think?"

"I don't know. Both?"

"There's still four more killers out there as far as we know and a whole lot more in the C.C.C."

"Well, that's up to the police now. I never should have gotten you involved in any of this. I'm so sorry."

Taylor touched his face and turned his head so he could look him in the eyes. "Hey. Technically, I got you involved in this. You were dealing with cheating husbands and shit until I paid you to find David."

"But when Eoin signed me on for the case, I dragged you with me."

"I don't drag, Paulie, though I do look good in an evening gown and heels, but seriously, if I didn't want to be a part of it, if I didn't need to be, I would have said no."

"Would you?"

"Yes."

Paulie put his hand on Taylor's wet, bare thigh. "Would you say no to me now?"

Taylor leaned forward and kissed him hard on the mouth. Then he pulled away and stood from the bed. "Yes," he said. "I don't want to fuck you because you're depressed and need an escape. I want to fuck you because you're happy and in love and want to be with me."

"In love?"

"Wishful thinking? Maybe it's not meant to be then. Partner's either way," Taylor said. He went to the dresser, opened the top drawer, and pulled out a pair of black boxer briefs, stepping into them. Then he opened the drawer below it and took out a folded pair of slacks, pulling them on one leg at a time. Then he turned around half-dressed and still shirtless. "We good?"

"Yeah, of course," Paulie said. "I just don't know if I can ever let this go if I can just move on knowing something like the C.C.C. is out there, targeting us, killing children. Case or no case, I have to keep trying to take them down, Tay."

"So let's do that then. We're P.I.s, Paulie. Let's go to some other town, some other city, and dig up dirt on more of the players, and keep going. We tried to do this with the institution, and we both ended up here with each other in this capacity. Now we can play by different rules, have purpose, and each other. We can do this."

Paulie nodded. "Yeah, okay." He nodded again. "Okay."

His cracked phone lit up and they both looked at it.

"Maybe we're not done after all," Taylor said, "Or it's a new job and a fresh start. Either way, you need to look at it."

Paulie sighed but he nodded. He got up and walked over, bending down to pick up the phone. Through the cracked screen he saw a text message from Miranda.

You didn't get this from me, but it felt wrong not to tell you. Madelyn Baker. 3492 Coconut Drive.

Paulie's eyes widened. He stared up at Taylor. "It's her. Janice. But if we go, we could get in serious shit, maybe even arrested."

"And if we don't, we'll never sleep again. Let me grab a shirt."

Paulie sighed. "We can't let her die. No matter what, we have to take her in, do this right."

"We will." Taylor shrugged a shirt on and began buttoning it.

"So we're really doing this?" Paulie said, stepping before him.

"It's the only thing we *can* do."

***

John wished he knew where to go, what to do, and how to find his partner. He couldn't just drive around to every abandoned building searching them one by one. Eoin could die before he finished, but he didn't know what else to do. He leaned on his car, smoking a cigarette and trying to think.

"Any ideas, kid?"

Turner shook his head. "Sorry, sir."

John licked his lips. He didn't want to get mad at the kid. It wasn't his fault. "Alright. I'm gonna bounce some shit off of you. Why, when there's a ton of players in this group all sharing their kill videos and helping each other off their local queers, and there's all manners of brutality on that fucking website, are all our vics stuffed in closets? Why do ours look like a serial job? Are they all done by the same person?"

Turner swallowed. "Maybe not but maybe they're all connected. The first guy was the real estate guy, right? You said the killer used his computer, yeah? Maybe they shared the info with the others. Maybe they were like all part of the same club or something? Is that stupid?"

John blew smoke out of his nose and shook a thick index finger at the young officer. "No, it's good. It's good. Maybe the C.C.C. wasn't the only group they shared together. What kind of group would they all be in though? I don't see some of them as book club people. Baking club? Knitting? What?"

His phone rang. John answered it in a hurry hoping it was news on Eoin. "Hey, Fratelli," Captain Marlowe said. "We got a call from a guy who claims to be Kyle's boyfriend. I need you to go talk to him."

"We already established Kyle was straight. He was giving it to my wife for God's sake. It's been a long time but I still remember what she looks like naked. No dick."

"Just talk to him. See what he has to say."

"These fucks have Murphy, Captain. I gotta find him."

"This is how you find him, Fratelli. Follow the leads. I've got guys going in all the places we've had on watch. If he's in one of them, we'll find him."

"Fuck. Fine. Tell me where to find him."

When John got the address, he hung up.

"Sorry about your wife," Turner said bashfully.

John glared at him. "Don't. Thank you...but don't."

"Got it."

"Come on. We gotta go question a guy. It might be pointless but we won't know until we get there."

"Yes, sir."

They got in the car. John paid a last glance to Eoin's vehicle. Then he pulled out and raced off with a squeal of tires.

Paulie parked in the Price Slashers grocery store parking lot. "It's up the block from here. I don't want to just pull up in front of the house and let her know we're coming. We'll walk up."

"What do we do if she's not home?"

"We wait until she is. She's gotta come back eventually."

They both checked their guns and got out of the car. Paulie stopped and looked at the front of the grocery store.

"What is it?" Taylor asked him.

"I just haven't been back to one of these places since... Never mind. Let's just go."

"Alright. Another time then."

"Yeah. Another time."

Side by side they headed off down the road.

***

John and Turner walked up to the young man sitting on the park bench. The guy was prettier than most of the women John knew and wore his makeup just as well. "Brandon?" John asked, walking up. The guy looked around nervously and nodded. "Why here?"

"Someone is killing us," Brandon said. "I-I didn't think they would in broad daylight in a crowded park."

"Alright. Listen. I don't have long. We have an emergency on our hands. What can you tell me?"

Brandon gave a subtle nod. He blinked to fight off the tears that would mar his perfect makeup. "Kyle and I had been together for two years but he wasn't ready for anyone to know. Once he finally tells someone he ends up dead."

The tears came anyway and Brandon dabbed at his eyes with a tissue.

"What about all the girls he brought around with him, brought to my house?"

"To your house?"

"Yes, I knew him personally. So I'll know if you're lying. Truth. Now." He saw the look on Turner's face and gave one back that said, "Later."

Brandon sighed. He looked at the painted nails in his lap. "It was all part of the ruse. He had success career-wise because women wanted him. It had to be believable but he said once he had enough money, and he felt the future was safe, we would be together for real, in the open. He did love me. He did."

"So who was the person he told?" Turner asked, earning him a look from John like he had overstepped.

"His sponsor."

"Sponsor? A queer sponsor? Like an alcoholic sponsor?"

"That's enough," John said, holding up a hand for Turner to stop. He looked at Brandon. "Please elaborate."

Brandon nodded. He took out Chapstick and rubbed it on his lips before nervously looking around at the surrounding trees. "There's a number. It's supposed to be anonymous. It's a local number too so it felt safe, real, you know? It's a support network for people in the closet."

John's eyes went wide. "Christ. Where did you find this number?"

"It was on flyers and business cards. They were all places queer people might be, the club bathroom, the coffee shop, the library, the college campus, always by the bowl of free condoms and flyers about AIDS awareness. It felt legit."

"But?"

Brandon shook his head. "I don't know. I saw it all the time but I never thought much about it because I'd been out since middle school, but one time after a couple of cayenne spice oat milk lattes, I got the number for Kyle. I thought maybe they would help him come to terms with things so we could be happy. He actually called and the sponsor he got was someone he already knew so he felt like he could trust her. It was a woman from his job, Trudy. She would talk to him and help him and even worked out fake girlfriends for him, but it didn't last long because he disappeared. If he was really killed for being queer, she had to have something to do with it."

John was frozen. He felt like the trees were closing in, the sky was falling, the ground was rising. He couldn't breathe. When he found his voice, he said, "You were brave to come forward under the circumstances. Do you still have that number?"

Brandon reached into a cute shoulder bag with a horned devil embroidered on it. When his hand came back, it was holding a card. He handed it to John.

"Alright. You've been helpful. Thank you for your time. Be safe getting home."

John turned and walked back to his car. Turner hurried to catch up to him. "What was that? What just happened?" he asked when they got back to the car.

"We found your club," John said to him as they got in the car and started it up. "A fake support network. I'd bet everything they all worked for it. It was a C.C.C. front business to identify people in the closet, to discover fresh victims."

"Jesus, that's horrible."

"It is. Listen, kid. You did a great job today. I appreciate your help, but I'm taking you back to the station."

"Huh? Why?"

"Because the next part is something I need to do alone."

***

"This is it," Paulie said, looking at the pastel green house with its well-manicured lawn and perfectly-trimmed bushes. "Car's in the drive. I don't know if it's hers but somebody is home."

"Alright. I'll go around the back in case someone tries to run. You take the front."

Paulie nodded. He hid behind a tree and watched as Taylor ran around the side of the house. Then he hurried to the driveway, his gun in one hand and a knife in the other. He stabbed the tires of the car just to be sure. He could deal with the consequences later. He wasn't letting this woman get away.

He went up to the front door then and knocked. "Madelyn Baker," he called. "This is Detective Paulie Paisano. I'm working with the police and I need you to open up."

To his surprise, the door opened.

20

J OHN PUSHED OPEN HIS front door. When he stepped inside his home, Trudy was at the kitchen sink wearing big pink rubber gloves and washing dishes. The whole place smelled of fresh-baked cookies. "What the fuck are you doing?" he asked as he shut the door behind him.

"What's it look like I'm doing? I'm washing dishes. You're home early. Everything okay?"

"Cut the bullshit, Trudy. You weren't fucking Kyle. What kind of world do we live in where it would be better if you were actually fucking him?"

Trudy sighed. She shut the water off and turned to face him. "Why don't you sit down and relax, have a beer? I made cookies."

John shook his head and drew his gun. He saw a flash of alarm go off in her face. Her gloves hand scooted over to a freshly washed knife in the dish drain. "Don't even think about it," he said. "You even reach for it and I'll shoot the hand off your wrist."

Trudy scowled. "I am your wife."

"Are you? I don't know who the hell you are anymore." With his free hand, he pulled out the card that Brandon had given him. "How the hell long have you been with these people, Tru? They kill people. Children. They kill fucking children."

"Oh for Christ's sake," Trudy said. She angrily poured herself a glass of red wine. "You're so preoccupied you're not just oblivious to me but the entire world around you. Do you not see what's happening? They're popping up everywhere like fucking mold spores, John! They're taking our children, our jobs, everything. They're converting people like it's a damn religion, convincing people it's not okay to be straight anymore. Do you know what happens if no one is straight, John? The human race fucking dies. Think about it. If all the Dicks fuck Dicks and the Janes fuck Janes, there will not be any more children. So we kill a few of their children now to protect the children of the future. You know how it goes, John. You can't make an omelet—"

"Stop!" he screamed. "I can't listen to this. You used to be good. You used to be good. I loved you."

"Past tense," she said, scoffing at him. "The world used to be good, John. This country used to be good, before this goddamn LGBT revolution. This is a war and we're not the ones who started it."

"I said shut up." He pointed his gun at her.

"You gonna shoot me? You gonna shoot your own wife over some damn queers?"

"If I have to. They have Murphy, Trudy. They've got my fucking partner."

"I told you he was queer."

"Where is he? How many people are in on your fake support network scam? Start talking."

She walked over and sat at the table sipping her wine. "Or what? No, I don't think I will."

"You know me," he said, walking over to her. "I don't believe in hitting women, but if there are lives on the line, which there are, I will knock the teeth out of your mouth if you don't start talking."

"Yeah, that sounds like police brutality, dear. You should really try the cookies. Homemade shortbread. They came out wonderful."

John snarled. He cocked the gun and pointed it at her face. "Where. Is. He?"

Trudy shook her head. "You're gonna shoot your own wife over some queer. I heard you assaulted some other officers. Internal affairs has already been notified."

"Oh yeah? Chris tell you that too, the dirty bastard? Holy shit. Is he involved in this? Is my wife and my crooked ex-partner in this shit together?"

"Well, now you just sound like a regular conspiracy theorist. "Can you please just calm down and listen to reason? John... Honey... It was always going to end this way. We tried to get her at the daycare and almost did but you showed up too soon. Ringold and Turner were supposed to delay you longer. Then you shot Janice."

"Her?"

"Oh come on, you know by now. Your partner isn't actually a man. She's just masquerading as one."

"You're a monster. Where is he?"

"I'm a monster? Your partner is practically Frankenstein. She mutilated her genitals and made them look like a man's. *That* is a monster."

John's lip twitched. He walked over and pressed the muzzle of his gun to her head. "I knew I hit her that day. Was she wearing a vest? Talk or I swear to God, I'll scatter your brains all over this fucking dining room."

"It was your vest, asshole. I gave it to her. You never need it because you're never dealing with big shit. You're a sham. Always were. You didn't even realize it was missing. Real fucking detective you are."

"That's the first thing you've said I actually believe. Now you need to tell me where Eoin is by the time I count to three or I'm going to kill you and find out another way. See, I know I've got time. You like to lock them in for days, to let them suffer."

Trudy smiled and sipped her wine. "Some of us do. Not Chris. He likes to beat 'em first, and lock 'em in the closet after just to make a statement."

"Conspiracy theory, my ass. Is that where he is, you psycho bitch? Does Chris have him?"

Trudy started laughing. She reached for her wine and he smacked her in the head with his gun. She dropped the glass and it shattered. One eye tightly closed she glared at him. "What the fuck, John? That fucking hurt."

His facial muscles twitched. "Oh, there you are. You done playing house now? Where the fuck is my partner?"

"I'm supposed to be your partner, you son of a bitch. We've been married more than half my life."

"Stand up and put your hands behind your back. Slowly. You're under arrest for conspiracy to commit murder. You have the right to remain silent."

As he continued to read Trudy her rights, she stood. "Fine. Cuff me. You'll never find him. At least I went down doing what was right and fighting for my country. More than I can say for your fat ass."

John put the handcuffs on her and she cried out. "That's too tight."

"Sounds awful. You can complain about it when IA comes to investigate me. Let's go. Out." He shoved her from behind. It was a surreal moment for John as he walked his high school sweetheart out of his home at gunpoint and put her in the back of his car. He got in the front with tears in his eyes and started the engine.

"This is what you get for being a fag hag," she told him. "You're fucked. She has him."

"Who?" he snarled as he pulled the car away from the curb into the road. "Who has him?"

"She does. Janice has him."

John slammed on the brakes and watched her fly forward and smack her head. He looked back at her, a thin stream of blood running from her hairline down between her eyes. "Who the fuck is Janice, Trudy?"

She smiled at him showing blood on her teeth as well. "We're all Janice," she said. Then she started cackling like a mad woman. John just put the gear in drive and drove off towards the police station.

***

"Hello again," Madelyn, known to many as Janice, said with a smile. "Please...come in."

Paulie stared at her. "Actually, I think you should come out. You're under arrest. There's no escaping it. We've got tons of evidence."

265

She whistled through her teeth. "Oof. That's a bit of a conundrum because we have your partner, who snuck around back. Got him as soon as he turned the corner. He didn't even have a chance to cry out. Sucker punches keep things quiet. So why don't you come in and we can talk?"

Paulie's eyes widened. Guilt seized his heart. He wanted to say screw the plan and put a bullet in this woman and be done with it but he didn't know who else was with her and how fast they would react in hurting Taylor. He didn't see any choice but to play along. "Alright. Back up but stay where I can see you," he said.

When she did as he asked, he stepped into the house. He wanted to avoid a sucker punch of his own. "I'm just going to close the door," she said, raising her hands defensively. She reached by him and shut the door. "This way."

She led him through the kitchen to an open door with a flight of stairs going down. "After you," she said.

"Like hell," Paulie told her. "You're going first."

"Not very trusting, huh? Okay. I'll go first if you give me your gun so I know you're not going to shoot me in the back."

Paulie didn't know the right thing to do. He didn't want to give her his weapon or have her at his back. He chewed on his lip. "Fine," he said, handing her his weapon.

She led the way down the stairs and he followed. When they reached the bottom they turned the corner and he saw Taylor on his knees, his mouth bleeding, and his arms tied behind his back. A man stood beside him with a gun pointed at the top of his head. It was a man Paulie recognized. "Captain Marlowe?"

266

Paulie grabbed Madelyn from behind. He put the knife he used to stab the tires of her vehicle to her throat as he reached around with his other arm and grabbed the wrist of her arm holding his gun. "Release it," he said firmly.

"Or what? He'll shoot your partner."

"And I'll slit your throat and we'll see who lives, him or me?"

"It's okay," Captain Marlowe said. "Give it to him."

She released the gun and Paulie took it. He kept her there though with the knife to her throat. "Now release Taylor. Send him over to me and I'll let her go and send her over to you."

"Or we both keep our prisoners for leverage and we talk," Marlowe said.

"Alright, talk," Paulie said.

"By now I'm sure you know that this is far bigger than a few bodies." Paulie stared at him but said nothing. The captain sighed. "We're trying to restore order."

"If you're part of this, why have you helped the investigation?"

"Think, Detective Paisano. Use those skills."

"You knew we were queer."

"Bingo," Captain Marlowe said, giving him a thumbs up with the hand not pointing a gun at Taylor. "I had Eoin hire you on so we could get you here to this moment. We got Murphy and Fratelli to split up so we could nab the tranny. I even got Miranda to text you the address after I called you and told you you were done. You should be mad at yourself for being so predictable."

Paulie looked horrified. He flinched when Marlowe mentioned Miranda.

"Oh, that hurt your feelings, did it? You thought Miranda was one of the good guys. Well, she is, but the good guys are not the side you thought. She will have already gotten rid of all that wonderful evidence you collected and put in one place so we wouldn't have to go dig it all up and race to dispose of it. That was very kind of you. I even helped John with his investigation. I insisted he talk to Kyle's boyfriend so he could realize that his own wife was one of us. That's what he gets for turning in one of our best. Chris was his own partner. Fratelli reported him to IA and a good man lost his job. That's when I recruited his wife to teach him a lesson. Soon, he will know how Chris felt."

Paulie smiled for the first time since he came down there. "That was stupid. Sure, learning the truth about his wife will hurt him, but it won't stop Fratelli from doing the right thing. You just said he turned in his own partner. He may be an ass but he's a good cop."

"Without a case. With no evidence. No wife. No partner. No helpful detectives. No proof. Nothing. He will realize he lost and it will break him. He is close to retirement anyway. It's over for him. It's over for all of you. And us, the C.C.C... We're just getting started."

"It's already hit the media. There's no way you get away with this," Taylor snapped from his knees beside the captain.

"One media outlet who works for the C.C.C. as well. We've already worked with them to craft a winning story, don't worry."

"There will be others," Paulie said. "Everyone has a blog or a vlog these days. Someone will be onto you."

"Not in this town. There's nothing for them to find. Sure they could become the next conspiracy theory nut, but a lot of good that will do. Why do you think there was no one at the school? The news goes where we tell them to."

"You're insane," Taylor barked through gritted teeth.

"Hey." Captain Marlowe slammed Taylor on the head with the butt of his gun. Taylor groaned and went down. "The world is insane. We're the ones trying to fix it."

Paulie pushed the knife enough to break the skin making a thin line of blood trickle from Madelyn's neck. "You hurt my partner and I hurt yours. Trust me, I'd love to hurt her."

"Of course you would," Marlowe said, "and then you pretend to be better than us. It's just proof that it's a kill or be killed world. I choose kill, and with that perfect segue, here are your options. You get in the closet willingly or we kill you first and then lock you in to make an artistic statement. What'll it be?"

***

John dragged Trudy into the precinct past a bunch of murmurs and giggles. He didn't give a shit anymore. He locked her in a cell himself and went to look for the captain. When he couldn't find him he went to Miranda and handed her the business card. "I need you to see how many of their phones have this number."

"What phones?" she said, brow furrowed.

"Or check their computers. You can do that right? This number is connected to the whole ring of closet murderers."

"Fratelli, what computers are you talking about?"

"All of them. What are you..." He looked at her face. "No. Come on. Fuck you. You can't be part of this. Not you."

"A part of what, Fratelli? What are you getting at?"

John shook his head. "They have Murphy locked in a closet somewhere, Miranda. Are you good with that?"

"Of course not. That sounds terrible. I'm sure we'll do everything we can to find him. He'll turn up eventually."

John sighed. "Fuck it." He drew his gun and pointed it at her. "Where is he? Where is Eoin Murphy?"

"Just a few days ago, you hated the queers just as much as we do. Did Murphy suck your dick or something?"

John snarled. He jammed the gun in her face. "Being too old to deal with ten million pronouns or dealing with the social media woke agenda does not equate to fucking killing people! You cannot do this! Where is Captain Marlowe?"

Miranda gave a bored sigh. "Who do you think is giving the orders, Fratelli? Come on. You really are a shit detective. It's probably time to just collect that pension and retire."

"Fuck you!" he screamed, spittle flying. He jammed his gun at her. "I won't try to blow the whistle. I won't try to ruin what you freaks have going. I just want my partner. Tell me where he is and we walk."

"By now, the others have let Trudy go and taken her somewhere safe. You've lost, Fratelli. It's over."

"What?"

He ran back to the cell to find it empty. "Where is she?" he shouted. "Where the fuck is she?" He stared at each and every cop that was there.

"Where is who, Fratelli?"

"You been drinking, Fratelli?"

"Fuck you!" John screamed. "Stop playing games. You saw me bring her in."

"Bring who in?"

"There's fucking cameras in here, dammit!"

He spun around and saw a smiling Miranda. "No there's not," she said.

"You can't do this!" John yelled, waving his gun around. "You can't fucking do this!"

"Do what, Fratelli?"

John screamed and ran out of the police station.

21

"I T'S DEFINITELY NOT GOING to end like this," Paulie said. "We're walking out of here together."

Captain Marlowe smiled. "It was always going to end like this."

Paulie heard footsteps behind him, movement. He kept the edge of the blade against Madelyn's neck and quickly glanced back toward the stairs. There was a man and a woman there, both armed.

"Satisfied?" the captain asked. "You can't win. Even if you do, you will be seen as murderers. The evidence of our wrongdoing gone, the only evidence will be of what you did to us in order to escape. Your lives will be over. No matter how you look at it, you lose."

Paulie looked at Taylor. He saw the look in his eyes. Willingly giving in to these people, allowing themselves to be killed just for being queer, was not an option.

***

John felt dizzy, lost, confused, and terrified. How could they have orchestrated all this and succeeded and he and the others just walked right into it? He couldn't stop thinking about Eoin locked in some closet somewhere, shitting on himself, and banging at the door. Scratching? Did they pull his fingernails out? Jesus.

Where the fuck are you?

He realized then that all the people who were supposed to be watching the abandoned buildings probably weren't watching them at all. *Nothing is real.* He chewed on his finger and tapped his gun against the side of his head.

Two men in suits approached him holding open wallets. "Mr. Fratelli? We're from Internal Affairs. We're going to need your gun and your badge please."

John shook his head. "Are you in on it too? Maybe not. What did they tell you? They've got my partner somewhere. I need help."

"Please don't make this more difficult, Fratelli. You've had a long, respectable career, but we've had several disturbing allegations against you recently and we need to investigate before you can return to active duty. Your suspension will come with pay but we're going to need your badge and your gun."

"You're not fucking listening to me. They're murderers. They have my partner."

"Where?"

"I don't know."

"Okay. We've listened to your counter-allegation and we'll investigate that as well, but we're still going to need your badge and your gun."

"This isn't right. He's going to die. Do you hear me? Murphy is going to die!"

"Please, Mr. Fratelli. If we have to call for backup this is going to get ugly and then it will be hard for us to salvage your reputation and the stellar years of service you've put in."

John was trembling. He handed his gun to one man and his badge to the other. Once they had them, they smiled at him and patted his shoulder. "The C.C.C. thanks you for delivering three dangerous queers into our net," the speaker said before they both walked away.

John fell to his knees in the street.

***

Paulie broke eye contact with Taylor. He knew there was only one way this could end now. He dragged the knife across Madelyn's throat and simultaneously dropped her while spinning around to fire his gun at the people behind him. As he did this, Taylor bit into Captain Marlowe's wrist tearing the flesh away with a spray of blood. The gun fell to the floor as the captain cried out and punched Taylor with his free hand.

The man and woman fired as well. A bullet caught Paulie in the shoulder and threw him into the wall as another pierced his side. The man caught Paulie's bullet in the neck, crimson spraying like a lawn sprinkler. He cupped a hand over it and fell back against the stairs. As Paulie slid down the wall leaving a trail of blood in his wake, he fired again, catching the woman between the eyes. Her brains blew out the back of her skull to coat the stairs.

Taylor lunged with his head driving the top of his skull into Captain Marlowe's belly and taking the wind out of him. As the man doubled over with a groan, Taylor took advantage of the close proximity and gnashed his teeth, ripping the nose off the man's face. He screamed in agony and fell. Taylor scrambled on his rear end through the blood pouring from Madelyn's opened throat, over to Paulie who lifted a trembling hand and cut the binds that held him.

When Taylor was free, they both looked up at the noseless captain standing over them. "You can't stop this," he said, his voice strange. "I'm just a single piece in a puzzle bigger than you can imagine."

Taylor took the gun from Paulie, raised it, and shot the captain in the heart. One perfectly placed bullet and he collapsed with nothing else to say. Taylor looked at Paulie. "Shit. We gotta go. We don't know how many more are coming."

"I know. Help me up."

"Oh shit. You're bleeding bad, Paulie. I gotta take you to the hospital."

"We can't. They're everywhere. That means the hospital too. When they realize who I am, they'll just finish the job. We have to leave town."

"Shit. Okay. Come on," Taylor said. He put Paulie's arm around his shoulder and he dragged him towards the stairs. A slowly dying Madelyn reached up at them feebly as they moved by her, blood still running from her wound. They slipped and slid in the brain matter on the steps and Paulie groaned in pain. "Sorry. Sorry. We're almost there."

When they got to the top they looked at the trail of blood and evidence they were leaving and realized just how right the captain had been. Their lives were over. The enemy was everywhere, hidden in plain sight and they had nowhere to go to escape them. Taylor laid Paulie in the passenger seat and then went around to the driver's side.

"They're gonna have an APB out on this car before long. We need to get somewhere fast," Paulie said weakly. He was sweating and bleeding in equal measure.

Taylor sighed as he started the car and drove away from Janice's house. "Okay. I have an idea. It's a crazy one but it's all we got. That ex I told you about, the narcissist who freaked me out? Chadwick? Well, he was a nurse and he doesn't like cops or well, anybody for that matter. He certainly wouldn't like people killing queers as he is one. I think he'll help. I hope so anyway. I don't know where we'll go from there but at least you'll be alive."

"Alright. Just go. Hurry."

"I will. Hang tight."

Taylor spit some of the captain's flesh that lingered in his mouth out the open window. He switched on the radio and Taylor Swift crooned, "Look what you made me do. Look what you just made me do," as he sped towards the interstate.

***

Sandra Matthews carried a basket of laundry down to the basement. She set it on the dryer. There were bangs and muffled screams from a door nearby. "My you're a loud one aren't you," she said as she loaded the clothing into the washer. "You can stop now. No one is going to look for you here, Detective Murphy. I already lost my son and now my husband got his brains blown out by his own brother. I'm a victim. You know what the funny thing is? Lance could be a prick sometimes but he loved that queer boy of ours. He never would have had the balls to do what I did. Well, I guess they're together now, right? You can join them in Hell too."

She dropped two soap pods into the washer, closed the lid, and started the cycle. It roared to life and shook and walloped. She grinned as the screams and commotion of her prisoner were now barely audible. Carrying the empty basket, she made her way back upstairs.

About the Author

Chisto is a bit of a mess, but he's okay with it. He learned how to survive and thrive by pouring himself into creativity. Since he was a child he's been writing, drawing, and making music. He is psychotically prolific and cannot keep up with his own brain.

Now he has a lot of books under his belt and a lot more coming. He's working on some more collaborations with some of his favorite authors and has around 300 stories in anthologies.

He works every convention he can afford to and loves to meet other authors and readers and lovers of horror and fantasy in general. He lives in NC with his fiancée, three kids, one dog, and a metric fuck ton of cats. He wants you to know that you're awesome and adorable and you should be proud.

If you're ever wondering if you deserve happiness, you do. If you ever wonder if you're worth it, you are. Also, you have a cute butt, but not as cute as his. Sorry, not sorry.